Almost Normal

By

Staz

Almost Normal

Copyright: 2020 by Staz

ISBN 978-1-7345634-1-2(ebook)

This is a work of fiction. Names, characters, business, events and incidents are the products of the author's imagination. Any resemblance to actual persons, living or dead, or actual events is purely coincidental.

All rights reserved. No portion of this book in whole or in part may be reproduced without express written permission from the author, except for brief quotations in reviews, articles, blog and social media posts.

About the Author

Staz is a former waitress, social worker, activity director, newspaper researcher, and elementary teacher. She is a traditional and self-published author. She currently dabbles in freelance writing and is the author of the blog, StoriesbyStaz.

Dedication

- Dedicated to anyone who has ever been a mother or a child

Chapter One

No one saw him coming as he slid across the highway that bright morning in late October. But in the time it took to slam on the brakes, turn the steering wheel, and let out a scream, death disguised as diesel fuel and eighteen wheels reached out and took my mother. On her way to teach four-year-olds how to finger paint and count to twenty, she was killed by a sleep deprived truck driver who had been on the road for almost thirty hours.

So here we are, dressed in stiff linen and silk at McComb's Funeral Home on Covington Road. I'm standing between my dad and my little brother, all of us next to the casket as the mourners pass by. Most of them are just empty faces, vague colors and shapes. I can't concentrate enough to focus on features or even care who they are, except for Angelica.

Angelica, my second cousin, was short, chubby and had cheeks like a Bulldog. She strutted up to me with an air of confidence that was unusual for an eight-year-old.

"Betsy, I'm sorry your mom died," she said, looking straight at me.

I wasn't sure, but I thought a piece of candy was matted in the side of her hair. She seemed so sure of herself, I didn't think she would have cared.

"I know you'll be sad when they close the lid on her," she said. "I was sad when they did that to my grandma."

Angelica passed by and a stream of cousins, neighbors, and friends walked past the coffin one by one, making sad faces, and insisting it would all get better with time.

"Each day the pain will be less," Aunt Casey from Toledo said. She was a bleached blonde with too much make-up. As far as I knew, she'd never closed the lid on anyone she'd been close to. What did she know about any of this?

The only one who had the nerve to tell me the truth was Tara Bethany, a foster kid who lived with our next-door neighbors.

"It's going to get a lot worse before it gets better," she said while cracking gum that smelled like it was a week old.

I just stared at her. She had bone straight black hair and overplucked eyebrows that surrounded her massive blue eyes.

"My mom died when I was nine and the first year majorly sucked."

"I'm sorry," I said in a whisper.

She nodded, and then said, "The only reason I'm telling you this is because no one else here will."

She moved on through the line and others followed behind her. But Tara, I couldn't stop staring at her. I'd never really paid attention to her before. All I knew was that she lived with Frank and Dorothy Atkins and that she was close to my age. Their children were grown and Dorothy had said that she thought it would be fun taking in foster kids. I wondered how much fun it was having someone like Tara around all day.

"I'm hungry," Joey said as soon as the last person in line was gone.

"Come on," Dad said, taking hold of my brother's arm while looking over at me. I followed them to a back room where more people were gathered around trays of food, a coffee urn, and a large pitcher of lemon-aide.

Dad didn't eat anything, but Joey ate everything in sight. He filled his plate with a ham sandwich, chips, brownies, and chunks of hot pepper cheese.

"He's old enough to remember everything but too young to understand," an old lady next to me said. Then she made a sad face and looked down at Joey.

I looked up and saw a bald guy nodding in agreement. His head was bobbing up and down like a wind-up toy. Then he said, "Between five and ten is always the worst age to lose a parent, and the poor boy is seven."

I wanted to ask him what the best age was to lose a parent, but I didn't want to waste the oxygen on him. Was fourteen good? Maybe fifteen? Who knew? I was halfway between both.

An hour later the showing was over and the three of us went home. But I had to get up the next day and come do it all over again at the funeral. If I would have known that the worst was still to come, that Tara really knew what she was talking about, I might have crawled into the coffin with my mother and closed the lid on both of us.

***

A week after the funeral, Dad called me into the kitchen and told me to sit down. It was a Sunday and I'd been sleeping late, dreaming of Mom when she was younger. I barely remembered her that way, but the dream had been so vivid. She was so beautiful, not a wrinkle or a blemish or a single gray root peeking through her ash blonde hair. I held onto that dream as long as I could, but Dad's voice had been too loud and persistent and her lovely face evaporated like a cloud.

Dad had called Joey, too, but that kid could sleep through a bomb blast. I sat down at the table and looked at Dad. He didn't look back for the longest time. Then he took a sip from his coffee cup. It seemed to give him the strength to look at me.

"Joey isn't going back to the Queen of Angels after Christmas," he said quickly. "And you won't be able to stay at Saint Augustine."

It took me a second to organize my thoughts. Christmas was several weeks away, but it was still a shock. "Why?" I managed to say.

He took another drink and cleared his throat. "Most of the money your mom made from her job was to send you and your brother to private school. We don't have that income anymore. Besides, the school doesn't provide transportation and with my work schedule I can't drop you off and pick you up in time."

Dad drove a truck for a soft drink company. He had to deliver soda to a dozen stores, and check and refill at least as many pop machines along the way. We'd either have to come to school too early or stay too late. There was no way he could get his entire route completed between eight-thirty and three-thirty.

Now I was the one who couldn't look at him. "Where will we be going to school?" I said, trying to think of all the Catholic schools in Fort Wayne. I was wondering if any of the others had before and after school care. I was still in denial, not yet ready to accept that the bottom had already fallen out.

He sighed and nervously twisted the mug in his hand. I could see the liquid swirling around inside. I wasn't sure what was in there, but it wasn't coffee.

"Probably Fairfield," he said, taking another drink. "And Joey will be at Crestview."

It was as hard for him to say it as it was for me to hear it. Shock and reality mingled together and settled into a knot in my stomach. The least he could have done was manage to send us to the Northwood Hills School District. It was a public school system, but was considered a good suburban district in a nice part of town.

We lived in a decent neighborhood, but our house was right on the edge of the city limits. We were on the great divide, that magical, unseen line between hope and despair. Less than a quarter of a mile from our house was the township line. If you lived on the east side, you went to school in Northwood Hills. If you lived a micro-second away on the other side, you went to school in the big urban district. We only lived a few blocks from the dividing line, but we might as well have lived in another galaxy. That was how different the schools were.

Chapter Two

The next week passed in a blur. I tried not to think about changing schools and decided not to tell anyone at Saint Augustine until it was absolutely necessary. Maybe it would never be necessary. Who knew what could happen between now and Christmas? Maybe Dad would win the lottery and I could forget I'd ever heard the word Fairfield. Maybe a tornado would crash through our house in the middle of the night and I'd never have to worry about going to school anywhere ever again. If I'd learned anything during the last month it was that the word *future* was as fragile as a puff of smoke.

After enduring the worst night's sleep I'd ever had in my life, I woke up the next morning to the sound of someone pounding on our front door. I got out of bed and looked at myself in the mirror. My auburn hair was so greasy and tangled I knew it would probably hurt to even run a brush through it. The skin around my mouth was chapped and crusty. But the worst were my eyes. They had always been a bright, almost emerald green. At that moment I was certain they were cloudy gray.

I shuffled across the living room and opened the door. It was Grandma Haynes. I figured she'd come to help clean the house or bring some groceries. It was a good thing, too. We needed all the help we could get. Her visit, however, wasn't what I expected. After I let her in, she seemed more annoyed because of our messy house than sympathetic.

"Where's your dad?" she asked, her hands planted firmly on her hips.

I glanced at the clock and saw that it was almost noon. "He's still in bed. He worked extra hours last night," I said without looking at her. I didn't lie very often and wasn't particularly good at it. If I looked straight at her, I was afraid she'd see it in my eyes.

Joey came running out of his bedroom. There was dried chocolate on his face and his hair hadn't been brushed in days. Grandma just frowned at him and looked away.

Sure, Dad was drinking too much, I wasn't helping around the house enough, and Joey was eating candy bars and chips almost every night. What did she expect?

"Are you kids eating regularly and is it good food?" she asked.

"Sure," I said. We were eating regularly and we thought it was good.

"Maybe I should prepare some meals for you," she said with a sigh.

I knew Grandma wasn't the type to make gooey desserts and cheesy casseroles. She'd bring over carrot sticks and broccoli delight.

"Really, Grandma, we're fine."

She sat down on the sofa and ordered me to sit next to her. She took hold of my hand and held it in her own. At least she was making an effort to be kind and understanding, but it wasn't working. Her hands were as icy as the glare in her eyes.

"I know you're grieving, but it's time to get back to the business of living and start taking care of things around here," she said without blinking an eye. "This has been just as much of a loss for me. She was my only daughter."

She had a point. But she hadn't been living with Mom. Her routine and everyday life hadn't been disrupted like ours had. She tried to smile but the corners of her mouth barely moved.

"Thanks for coming by. I'll tell Dad you were here," was all I could manage to say.

***

The first day of December I woke up to a dark, dreary morning. I looked out the window and the sky seemed to surround the house like a dirty wool blanket. Low lying clouds had covered the sun for nearly a week. No wonder I'd been so tired and wanted to sleep all the time. We were living in perpetual twilight.

I thought I heard the phone ring, my dad's footsteps, and then mumbling in the dark. I leaned over and looked at the clock on my dresser. I was shocked that it was already ten. I crawled out of bed and stumbled through the living room like a zombie in my own house. My back hurt and my leg muscles ached from lying in bed so long.

It took a few minutes for my brain to start functioning again. But when I realized school had started over an hour ago, I ran to Dad's bedroom in a panic. He was still in his pajamas. I saw an empty wine bottle on the floor by his bed.

"Why didn't you wake me up?" he said without looking at me. "My alarm didn't go off."

"Mine didn't either," I said. "Or else I slept through it."

"Get your brother up and get him ready or you're going to miss school," he said.

Fifteen minutes later we were all in the car and speeding toward Queen of Angels. After dropping off Joey, he pulled out of the parking lot and headed toward Saint Augustine where I was a freshman.

"Have you told them yet?" Dad said before we pulled into the school parking lot.

"Told them what?" I asked, pretending that I didn't know what he was talking about.

"That you'll be starting Fairfield in January."

I didn't realize at the time that it was strange for a parent to expect a kid to tell the school they were leaving that they weren't coming back. I only knew that I dreaded doing it. As long as no one else knew, it didn't seem real.

"Let me have Christmas," I said as Dad stopped in front of the big double doors. "Once they know I'm leaving I won't be able to enjoy the dance and all the parties in the same way."

Dad didn't say anything for several seconds. "I suppose you can wait until after Christmas," he finally said. "The semester doesn't end until the second week of January anyway."

"Thanks," I said while getting out of the car.

I hurried up to the front of the school and walked past the ornate statues of saints and angels that had been donated through the years and had grown to quite an elaborate collection. As soon as I walked through the double doors, I saw the grand statue of Mary looking down at me as she had done every day since the beginning of school.

I'd always believed I was safe between the pristine walls that Father Henderson insisted were guarded by angels. Death and debt and drunken nights couldn't harm me there. The moment I left, I now sensed that it would all follow me like a dark mist.

***

I was glad when Christmas was finally over. It was a holiday I no longer recognized. Joey and I spent Christmas Eve with Grandma Haynes. We ate a late dinner, opened presents, and then went to Midnight Mass before she brought us home. The next morning I woke up around ten and went out to the living room.

Our Christmas consisted of a tiny tree from the dollar store and a few shabbily wrapped presents stuffed carelessly underneath. I felt guilty being angry. I knew plastic trees and presents wasn't what the holiday was all about, but it was what the plastic tree and cheesy presents represented that got to me -- a dad who no longer cared enough to even make an effort.

A week later when New Year's came around, I felt just as disillusioned. I'd asked my best friend, Olivia, to spend the night. Her mom wouldn't let her and I was stuck spending the evening with Joey. There was something about having a mom in the house that made everyone feel safe. I could already see my friendship with Olivia slipping away and I hadn't even started Fairfield yet.

Dad hadn't said anything about going out, but all afternoon on New Year's Eve day he seemed nervous.

"Where are you going?" Joey said as he stood next to Dad in the bathroom, watching him put gel in his hair.

Instead of answering, Dad squeezed gel into Joey's hair so he could make it spiky and stick out all over the place. From where I was sitting in the living room, I could see Dad walk into his bedroom and stand in front of the dresser mirror. For the next ten minutes I watched as he pulled shirts out of his closet and held them up in front of the mirror like a teenage girl unsure of what to wear. That was when I knew Dad had a date.

Two hours later he announced that "Abbie" and some friends from work had pulled into the drive. All three of them came into the living room together. Dad's friend from work and his wife stood together in front of the coffee table. The other woman stood next to Dad, nervously twisting her dirty blonde hair around her finger.

"These are my kids, Betsy and Joey," he said, pointing us out as he said our names. Like she wouldn't have already known which one of us was Betsy and who was Joey?

"They're so cute," she said, like we were a couple of dolls propped up on a shelf. She leaned over and tapped Joey on the nose and I could smell the sickening mixture of cigarettes and cheap perfume.

"We're going to see a movie," Dad said, his hand behind the small of her back.

"Your daughter is pretty," she whispered into Dad's ear, loud enough that she knew I could hear.

This was so phony, trying to butter up the new boyfriend and his stupid kids so she could horn her way into his life. If she would have had the guts to say Joey's hair looked like a bird's nest and that the zits on my forehead were totally gross, I might have given her a chance.

"She's nice," Joey said, peeking between the curtains as they got into the car. He was seven. What did I expect?

Joey and I ate pizza and watched the ball drop in Times Square at midnight. It was almost three before I heard Dad come in. I'd fallen asleep on the couch, warm and snug under a pile of pillows and blankets. The opening of the front door woke me, but I didn't get up. They were giggling when they came inside, and this time it was just Dad and Abbie. They stopped on the other side of the sofa and started talking. Obviously, they hadn't seen me, but I could see their shadows on the wall and hear their soft, muffled voices.

"Better not," I heard Dad say, his voice sounding louder and more serious. "I'll call you tomorrow."

Surely, she didn't ask to spend the night, I thought. They'd only had one date.

Chapter Three

I started the second semester of my freshman year at Fairfield High School the day after an ice storm. There was still a splattering of freezing rain when Joey and I left for the bus stop. The high school bus was scheduled to come fifteen minutes before the one for elementary kids, but there were several other kids from the neighborhood who would still be waiting with Joey after I was gone so I assumed he'd be okay.

I'd never rode a school bus before in my life. Mom had taken me to school every day in a mini-van with plush leather seats. Whenever I complained it was too hot or too cold, Mom would always adjust the temperature. And if I didn't like the song that was playing on the radio, she would change the station. When I saw that big yellow bus barreling through the ice and gravel and dreariness of a Monday morning I almost started crying.

When bus thirty-one finally came to a screeching stop, I climbed on after a girl with red hair and a boy who looked too old to be in high school. All the windows were closed and the bus smelled like dirty laundry. The kids who got on before me sat down right away but I didn't know where to go. There weren't very many places left and I just stood there.

A boy sitting a few seats back from where I was standing yelled out, "Just sit down. The seats are all the same."

I suppose he was right about that and since the driver had already started taking off, I plopped down in the closest open spot, next to a girl eating a Snickers bar. In the time it took her to finish the candy bar and get most of the way through a bag of chips, the driver had pulled up to the entrance of Fairfield High School.

Just getting off the bus and pushing my way through the crowd scared me. I was pulled into a sea of people so deep I feared I might drown before I got to the front doors. I had a schedule of classes but not a clue where any of them were. I was tardy for my first two classes and the one right after lunch.

The next few days were like living in a hazy dream. None of it seemed real. I was certain that at any moment I would wake up and Sister Kate would be standing over my desk with a scowl, waiting for me to recite the Lord's Prayer or the Quadratic Formula or whatever she demanded at that particular moment.

By the end of the first week I finally ran into Tara, the foster kid who lived with the neighbors. It was the first time I'd seen her since the funeral. She was sitting on the bleachers when I came into gym class.

"You're the girl who lives with Dorothy Atkins, right?" I said as she stared at me, trying to remember who I was. "You were at my mom's funeral. Your name is Tara."

She looked impressed that I knew her name, then suddenly remembered where she was. She wasn't at a funeral around a bunch of people she'd probably never see again. She was at high school, and any sort of sentiment would be perceived as weakness.

"It's me," she said, leaning back casually on her elbows.

"Are you supposed to be in this gym class? I haven't seen you here all week."

She laughed. "Yeah, I'm in this class. But I was suspended for three days."

I didn't ask what she'd been in trouble for. Tara was the type of person that if she wanted you to know she'd be sure to tell you. And if she didn't want you to know, you were probably better off not asking.

***

When I got home from school, Abbie, the woman Dad had gone out with on New Year's Eve, was already there. As far as I knew he'd only gone out with her once or twice since then, but here she was, wiping down the kitchen and rearranging dishes in the cabinets. I could smell cookies in the oven. Dad must have given her a key to the house, which surprised me since he'd only known her a few weeks.

"Chocolate chip or sugar?" she said with a big syrupy smile. She pulled two trays of cookies out of the oven and carefully set them on the counter by the stove.

The cookies actually looked pretty good, but I only took one. I didn't want to encourage her. Joey, on the other hand, was young enough that he could be bought with a few batches of cookies and a fake smile. When he got home he devoured five cookies and two glasses of milk in about ten minutes.

Abbie stood over him, watching adoringly as he ate, as if she actually enjoyed watching someone else's kid smear chocolate across his face and spill milk down his shirt.

She eventually noticed my lack of interest in her homemade cookies and redirected her attention back to me. "What's your favorite meal?" she asked.

My favorite meal was spaghetti and meatballs, but I didn't want to make it easy for her. "Cantonese Chicken," I said, remembering I'd read it once off a Chinese menu. "And Singapore style egg rolls. The sauce not too spicy," I added.

She looked at me like I'd just asked her to butcher a cow and serve up the intestines. "Maybe we can order out for that," she said stiffly.

For a second I was afraid she'd actually do it and I'd have to choke down a couple of egg rolls and Cantonese Chicken. But she never asked me about food again.

After that Abbie was at our house almost constantly. She did laundry and read to Joey. I knew she was dead serious about worming her way into our lives for good when she cleaned the downstairs bathroom. But even Abbie couldn't get Joey to bathe or brush his teeth regularly. The truth was she didn't care if he was properly cared for or not, just that he liked her.

On a Friday night she showed up with a bottle of wine for Dad. If only she knew he'd already drank half a bottle an hour earlier, she wouldn't have bothered. He was already in a woozy, feel-good state of mind. Then Dad muttered those words I heard in my sleep now -- "Take Joey in his room and keep him busy."

We stayed in there about forty minutes reading and playing with the Lego set. As soon as he said he was hungry, I saw my excuse and went out to see what they were doing.

They were in the kitchen playing two-handed Euchre, laughing and sipping their wine.

"What do you need?" Dad said as soon as he saw me.

"Joey's hungry. We didn't have dinner," I said. Without looking away from his hand full of jacks and aces, he dug his wallet out of his back pocket and flipped it open with one hand.

"Here, take a twenty and order something from Waiter on the Way," He said. He was showing off in front of Abbie, pretending that he was always opening his wallet with one hand and letting us order anything we wanted.

I felt like grabbing more than a twenty and ordering food from all over town. I reached in and pulled. I got a twenty, a five, and two ones. I ordered two kinds of pasta, a large salad and extra bread sticks from my favorite Italian restaurant. I took the food into Joey's bedroom, set it out on the floor, and we gorged ourselves.

When I woke up the next morning and saw her car in the drive, I knew she'd spent the night. The thought of her sleeping in Mom's bed made me sick. As I sat by the window, I saw a few of my folders from last semester stuffed under the bed. I pulled the top one out and started looking through it. On one side of the folder was a map of the United States and notes on the American Revolution. On the other side were papers about the great patriarchs of the Bible. Father Henderson taught both History and Religion.

He always liked to compare our own lives to Biblical events, like Moses and the Israelites crossing the Red Sea to get away from Pharaoh and slavery. He said at some point we would all have our own Red Seas to cross. He explained that some people only had a few Red Seas in life to get through, while others, unfortunately, had a lot more.

Last year he told us about a man he counseled who didn't make it across. He drowned in a sea of drugs and despair, waves of Crystal Meth and cheap Heroin sweeping him under before he made it to the other side. He said the miracle wasn't just that the Red Sea parted; but that it stayed open long enough for all of them to cross over. He said when people drowned in their own Red Sea it wasn't because God wouldn't open the way for them, but because they lost faith and gave up before getting to the other side.

But I thought what had happened to me was more like a shipwreck. There wasn't anything I needed to escape from or anything I'd been wandering through. My catastrophe had been sudden and unforeseen. I'd been sailing along on an ocean liner, a luxury yacht with all the comforts a fourteen-year-old could ask for. And like the Titanic in the cold of the Atlantic, we had gone down without warning. Now here I was, clinging to pieces of debris, grasping anything floating by I could grab hold of to keep from drowning.

"Is there anything I can help you with?" Father Henderson had asked a few weeks after Mom had died. I wanted to tell him I had a thousand questions, but I knew he couldn't answer any of them. Instead I just smiled and shook my head.

Chapter Four

After about a week I was used to riding the bus, at least in the morning. Most of the kids were sleepy and it was pretty quiet on the way to school. The ride home in the afternoon was another story. Maybe it was the high carb and sugar content in the school lunches. Maybe it was the after-effect of 2,000 hormonal bodies all packed in over-crowded classrooms for six hours. Whatever the reason, the contrast between the morning and the afternoon was amazing. And the bus driver did nothing to try to curb the chaos.

The kids in front of me had been yelling and throwing things since the bus left the school. When one of the girls sitting on the end turned around, I tried not to act surprised. She had a scar across her left cheek that looked pretty recent.

"Are you from Sycamore Hills?" she said.

Sycamore Hills was the richest neighborhood in Fort Wayne. Most of the people who lived there were millionaires.

"No," I said, sounding offended. "Would I be on this bus if I lived in Sycamore Hills?" Being from that neighborhood would have meant getting beat up on a regular basis. Then I realized that telling anyone I'd come from a private Catholic school probably wouldn't fare much better.

"You look like a chick whose dad lost a bundle in the stock market and now you're slumming it," she said.

"I'm a chick whose mom died and now I'm slumming it," I said stiffly.

She didn't say anything after that. Sudden death had the power to silence all the critics.

Even though there were a lot of rough kids on this bus, thankfully the worst bullies didn't ride number thirty-one. There were several kids with violent reputations at Fairfield, but supposedly the worst was Dani Thompson.

My first day at Fairfield I'd heard of Dani, though I didn't actually see her for another week. I'd been told by at least a dozen people what a beast she was, a sophomore who stood as tall as most of the male teachers and weighed at least as much. But she wasn't fat. Solid, huge, massive were all words used to describe her, along with other less friendly terms like treetop, stump legs, and gorilla mutant.

It was rumored she liked to start fights for no reason at all. She supposedly beat up kids for taking the last piece of apple pie in the cafeteria or using the last piece of toilet paper in the restroom.

Before I saw her, I had this picture in my mind of what she looked like, an image I became certain she couldn't possibly live up to. I was wrong. The first time I saw her was during a pep assembly on a Friday afternoon. I couldn't quite put my finger on what it was that made her so frightening. Maybe it was her large stature, enormous hands, or wide set eyes. Or maybe it was because she was beating up some girl under the bleachers while the pep rally was in progress.

While each of the varsity basketball players were being introduced, I peeked through a crack in the bleachers, along with about twenty other kids. Dani could swing a left hook like a seasoned prize fighter and she was quickly beating some skinny girl to a bloody pulp.

"Go get a teacher!" a lone voice cried.

I couldn't tell if the voice came from under the bleachers or up here with us.

"You do and you'll be next!" Dani warned, momentarily looking up. There was blood streaming down her face. I could only imagine what the other girl looked like.

I glanced over at the group of teachers standing by the gym doors, only about twenty feet away. Not one of them turned and looked this way. They kept pretending not to hear the desperate cries of a girl getting beat senseless. They smiled and clapped while the cheerleaders formed a human pyramid in the center of the gym.

It was awful that they weren't willing to help, but I understood why. It was almost two on a Friday afternoon. In less than an hour they would be gone for two glorious days. If one of them even turned their head and acknowledged the suffering it would mean hours of filling out papers and making phone calls and dealing with uncooperative parents. I wouldn't have looked either.

I was surprised when I saw the girl walk out from under the bleachers on her own steam. She could walk but that was about it. Blood dripped from her nose, her mouth, her arms. No one acted like she even existed until she made it to the principal.

With blood dripping on his brushed leather loafers and Canali blazer he could hardly keep pretending she wasn't there. He whisked her out of the gym and down the hall toward the nurse's office. In spite of what had just happened, the pep rally went off without a hitch.

I could only remember one physical fight in all my years of attending Catholic school. When I was in the fifth grade a couple of eighth grade boys got in a fight out on the playground. No one got to go to recess for the rest of the day and the next morning we had a special assembly with Father O' Malley discussing the importance of loving our neighbor and turning the other cheek. If everything stopped at Fairfield each time some kid beat somebody up nothing would ever get done.

The next week I finally had my first close up and personal encounter with Dani when she was transferred to my third period World Geography class.

"She never does any work, never turns in homework and is always the first one done with tests because she just circles answers without reading the questions," the girl who sat beside me said. She'd been in two classes with Dani the year before.

"Dani doesn't do anything in any of her classes, unless she thinks it's fun," the girl said. "Just make sure you stay out of her way."

I nodded. I knew what she meant. In a big public school it was easy to get off on the wrong foot and make enemies without even realizing it. I learned not to make direct eye contact with anyone or stare too long at any of the attractive boys. If any of the girls thought you were trying to make a move on their boyfriend, they'd take their revenge in the restrooms or in the halls where the cameras couldn't see them. But I knew if Dani decided she didn't like you it would be nearly impossible to stay out of her way. And she decided pretty early on she didn't like me.

A few days later the lady in the lunchroom picked me to be a lunch helper. This meant I got to leave World Geography early each day to wipe down tables and set out the food trays. It only took Dani two days to figure that out.

"How come that stuck-up, prissy girl gets to leave ten minutes early every day?"

"That's not of your business," I heard the teacher say as I walked out of the room.

Later that day I saw Dani coming toward me as I was trying to get books out of my locker. She grabbed me from behind and slammed me against the lockers so hard my lungs hurt when I gasped for breath.

"You ain't nothing special cause your mama died," she said.

"I didn't say I was," I said, trying to sound tough.

"I know that's why they gave you cafeteria duty," she said making a fake sad face, "Cause the little Catholic girl's mommy died."

I saw a documentary once about women in prison. Through an underground line of communication, the inmates knew everything about the new convicts coming in, even before they got there. There must have been a system like that in big public schools because Dani seemed to know a lot about me.

"I didn't ask for cafeteria duty. They gave it to me."

"Maybe, but you acted like you was something special when you strutted out of class early."

She was sticking her large face right into mine. Her breath smelled like the sausage pizza we had for lunch.

"I just do what they tell me," I said. "I don't have a choice." A girl like Dani hated helplessness, but she understood it.

"Just remember, you're no different than the rest of us."

"But it is different for me," I whispered after she finally let go and walked away. I knew I didn't belong here, that it wasn't supposed to end up this way.

Chapter Five

As soon as Dad walked in the door that evening, I could hear him on his phone with Abbie. Just hearing her voice through the phone irritated me.

"So is Abbie going to be hanging around here all the time now?" I said as soon as he was off the phone.

He looked at me like I had a lot of nerve even asking something like that.

"Abbie is a nice lady. You need to show her some respect."

I wanted to do what Joey did when he thought something was ridiculous. He made a spitting sound for ten seconds straight. But I was much better at rolling my eyes and letting out a huffy sigh.

"You're slumming it with Abbie, especially after being married to Mom," I said.

His eyes widened and his head tilted to one side. He was as surprised as I was that I'd actually said that. "Your mom was no saint," he said, wagging a finger at me.

"What's that supposed to mean?"

"Believe me, I'm not slamming your mom. It's just if you knew the truth about her maybe you'd realize she was human like the rest of us and give Abbie a chance." He opened the fridge, grabbed a bottle of wine and headed for the recliner in the living room. He knew I wouldn't let it go after hearing something like that.

"What *truth*?" I said. I stood right in front of him, blocking his view to the TV.

Even though he tried to look at me with an intense stare his eyes were muddy and unfocused, but his words were as sharp as a sword. "I'm not sure your mom's death was an accident. She may have been so depressed that she drove into that truck on purpose."

Before my mind could even process what he said my mouth shot back a rebuttal.

"That's a lie! She'd never kill herself!" I screamed.

He shook his head, clutching the bottle between his legs like a life preserver in choppy seas. "She suffered from clinical depression for years, but did everything she could to keep you kids from knowing how difficult things were for her."

"She was never depressed around me," I said defiantly.

He took a quick swallow. "She painted that face on for you and your brother. But you're old enough to know now."

"If that's true, prove it." I was so certain he'd never produce any evidence that I called him a coward and a liar when he got up and left the room. I heard him in his bedroom opening drawers and tossing things around.

A few seconds later he came back out, the wine bottle in one hand and what looked like a prescription bottle in the other. He set the small bottle on the coffee table and then fell back into the recliner. This time he took a long, slow drink and then stared at the bottle on the table. "Go ahead, look at it," he said.

I hesitated before picking up the bottle. I wasn't sure what the name of the medication was. It was a long word, with generic written next to it. But it was prescribed for Kathleen Kimmel, to treat depression and anxiety.

"That still doesn't mean she killed herself," I said. I threw the bottle on the floor and stomped off to my bedroom.

***

By the beginning of February, Dad and Abbie were together almost every night. She hadn't technically moved in but I realized she'd changed tactics. Instead of coming right out and discussing it, she'd just spend so much time over here that it wouldn't make any difference if she officially moved in or not.

Each time she came over she'd bring another item of clothing, another pair of shoes, an extra toothbrush, until she had almost as many things in the closet and bathroom as Dad. Since she still hadn't completely penetrated our inner circle, she kept trying to be extra nice to me and Joey.

"I'm so sick of winter," she said on a Saturday afternoon while we were all sitting around watching TV. "Why don't we have an indoor picnic?" she said excitedly.

Why don't we? Because that's stupid, I wanted to say. But I didn't want to be the killjoy, so I waited to see what Joey said.

"That sounds like fun!" he said, practically shouting.

"We can grill hamburgers and hotdogs on the back porch," she said. "I'll make potato salad and we can spread a blanket out on the living room floor."

She had a goofy smile on her face and Joey giggled. A few hours later we were all having a picnic in the living room. Abbie was relishing the role of little Miss Homemaker. But I knew it was all a facade, and as the evening wore on, she and Dad would drink enough that she would leave the homemaker gig behind and turn into something else entirely. Go-go dancer and female escort were two words that came to mind. But for now, I had to put up with a bunch of sappy mother hen nonsense.

"More mustard or ketchup?" she said sweetly as she stared adoringly at Dad.

What was she going to do? Squeeze it on the bun for him like he was two?

"A little more mustard would be nice," Dad said.

I almost threw up when she pulled the bun off his hamburger and squeezed it on. Mom never would have done anything like that.

Abbie was such a chameleon. She knew had to mold and transform herself in a thousand different ways, adapting to whatever situation she found herself in. Considering everything that had happened to me, I could probably learn something from a woman like Abbie. But I wasn't ready yet to accept that this was the reality of my life. I wasn't ready yet to adapt and transform. I still harbored lovely illusions of escape, that my current state was only temporary. But after what happened the following night, I knew I'd better get used to it.

Dad was always telling her not to smoke in the house, and to at least go out on the porch when she did it. Sometimes she went out there, but most of the time she didn't.

I was watching some old game show on the cable channel when I got a whiff of what smelled like burning marshmallows on an open campfire. The soft blanket wrapped around my legs and the quiet din of the television must have lulled me into a state of oblivion because for a minute all I did was inhale that warm, sweet aroma.

Then Joey came running into the living room. "Something is burning in the kitchen," he said, wrinkling his nose.

I jumped up off the sofa. Cooking in the house was nearly nonexistent. That's when I knew something was wrong. Before I had a chance to follow the smell, Dad ran out of the bedroom with a bath towel wrapped around his waist.

"Get out of the house!" he ordered. "Go to the Atkins and call the fire department."

Joey was fully dressed but I was in a T-Shirt. I stumbled through the living room, pulling on a pair of sweat pants. I grabbed Joey's hand and ran out the front door.

When Dorothy let us in I don't even remember what I told her, but it must have been coherent enough that she understood what was going on and knew to call the fire department.

She opened the door to the garage. "Frank!" she yelled. "Go across the street and make sure Mr. Kimmel is okay."

That's when I screamed, "Dad! I've got to go get my Dad!" But she pushed me down in a kitchen chair, and by then Frank was already on his way.

Dorothy wouldn't let us go to the front room to see if our house was up in flames or not. She set out a little tray of fruit for Joey and made us stay in the kitchen. It was almost like she was entertaining. She was setting out snacks while the neighbors' house burned down.

Then I saw Tara. She was sitting on the sofa, casually eating popcorn out of a Tupperware bowl. *It's going to get a lot worse before it gets better* stuck in my brain like a bad drug. She looked at me the moment I thought of those words and I hated her for being right.

But she didn't gloat about it. She came in the kitchen and offered Joey and me some popcorn. I took a handful and watched her. She acted as if everything I was going through she'd already experienced and knew how it would turn out.

"You don't like that Abbie chick much, do you?" Tara said.

"Not particularly. How can you tell?"

"For starters, most kids don't like their dad's new squeeze, especially after their mom dies. Besides, as much as you were worrying about your dad, you didn't seem too concerned if she went up in a ball of flames."

I felt naked and exposed in front of Tara. I could hide anything I wanted from adults, but she had the ability to crawl inside my brain and connect all the dots.

"I really don't care one way or the other," I said, trying to act cool and detached, the way she always did. But I knew she didn't buy it.

An hour later, after a fire truck and a police car had come and gone, Dad came over and told us it was okay to come home.

It turned out there was quite a bit of smoke and fire damage in Dad's bedroom, but not much in the rest of the house. He said insurance would pay for the repairs, and since it was an accident there was no need to bring it up again. That's when I knew the fire had been Abbie's fault.

The next day we had a two-hour delay and the bus didn't come until almost ten. After both Dad and Abbie left that morning, I decided to call the police. I asked for the officer who had been in charge of investigating Mom's accident. He wasn't on duty that day, but I left a message that I had some questions about the accident and that I wanted him to contact me. I didn't believe for a second that she'd committed suicide, but I had to know for sure.

Chapter Six

My best friend from Saint Augustine, Olivia, turned fifteen the day after Valentine's Day. She invited me to come over the following Saturday. I had been looking forward to it all week, but when I found out that Olivia had also invited Marla Benson, I canceled at the last minute. I didn't want some girl tagging along that before I'd left we had barely given the time of day to. It was obvious that Marla was her new best friend.

Watching your best friend slip away was like letting go of a helium balloon. Once you had let go there was nothing you could do but watch it get smaller and smaller on the horizon until it completely disappeared. It was easier just not to see her at all, than to sit around and listen to the two of them talk about things I wasn't part of anymore.

On Monday I was still so depressed about what happened with Olivia that I was aimlessly wandering through the halls between classes, not following my usual routine. I usually made an effort to avoid Dani whenever I could, but today I forgot all about her and walked right by her locker on the way to study hall.

Just as I passed by Dani's locker a voice behind me yelled, "I smell gorilla meat!"

I spun around and saw an impish girl with tight red curls grinning like a Cheshire cat.

But the moment I looked into her eyes she disappeared in the crowd.

"What did you say?" Dani demanded as she grabbed hold of my arm with one of her massive hands. She could have broken my arm with little effort if I hadn't instinctively pulled away. Dani was big and powerful, but she wasn't fast.

"I didn't say it! I swear I didn't!" I yelled back as I ran for my life.

As I sprinted down the hall other kids shouted, "Run! She's right behind you!" But as soon as Dani would pass them, they would yell, "Go get her! Kill her!"

I rounded the corner and headed toward the main entrance. By the time I made it to the front office Dani wasn't chasing me anymore.

At lunch I saw the girl who had been right behind me when she yelled at Dani. She was in the ala carte line in the cafeteria. I was four kids behind her, watching as she dug her fingers into a sandwich. After that she picked up a handful of fries and then tossed them back down. A cafeteria lady yelled at her and then threw out the fries she had touched, but someone bought the sandwich.

I'd never known anyone with such an intense stare. I wondered if it was natural or rehearsed. I put a few things on my tray, paid for them, and followed her to a table.

"You're the one who called Dani gorilla meat," I said, looking right at her.

She popped a tator tot in her mouth and grinned. Then she said, "*I smell gorilla meat*," in a deep, frightening voice that didn't match her face. I should have been mad. But what was I going to do about it? Especially now, standing in front of her like a zombie, holding a tray full of chicken nuggets, tator tots, and a carton of apple sauce.

"Take a load off and sit down," she said. "I'm Mary Frances."

"My name is Betsy Kimmel," I said, sitting down across from her.

"You're new here, aren't you?"

I nodded and opened my milk. "Yeah, and I've already made an enemy in Dani Thompson."

"I'll tell you what," Mary Frances said, swallowing her food and shaking a finger at me. "If Dani ever comes after you again and I'm around, I'll take care of her for you."

I didn't believe that for a second, but there was something interesting about Mary Frances that made me want to talk to her. "What grade are you in?" I asked.

"Freshman," she said.

I was shocked. She seemed too proud, too in control of herself to only be a freshman. Mary Frances and I spent the rest of lunch together, but I could never see myself getting to be good friends with her. Maybe she could be an in-the-meantime kind of friend, a diversion along the way until someone I could really connect with came along.

***

Grandma Haynes was supposed to pick me up after school on Wednesday for an eye doctor appointment. I wasn't sure why Grandma was taking me. She never offered to do anything for us.

I waited in the office until almost four. When the secretary started clearing her throat each time she looked at me, I knew she was getting irritated.

"How about I call your dad?" she said with a fake, sympathetic voice.

"Did my grandma call?" I said. "She's the one who is supposed to pick me up."

"I can check with the Assistant Principal, but I don't think so."

She got up and walked to Ms. Ashbury's office, her heavy frame knocking into the file cabinet and the corner of the desk. From where I was sitting I could see them with their heads together, whispering and occasionally looking my way. Finally, Ms. Ashbury informed me that no one was coming to get me.

"Your grandmother won't be coming," she said. "A lady in her retirement complex got sick and your grandmother took her to the hospital."

Then she sighed, sounding more annoyed than concerned for some old lady who was screwing up everyone's afternoon schedule because she had the nerve to get sick.

So much for the eye doctor, I thought. I didn't want to go anyway. His assistant wasn't very friendly and they always put stuff in my eyes that made them burn.

The Assistant Principal had a meeting that started in a few minutes and the secretary couldn't stay past four-thirty. Since the band instructor was still in the building, I was told I'd have to wait in his room until Dad got there. I grabbed my backpack and followed Ms. Ashbury through the empty halls to the east end of the building.

The band room was a universe all its own. The high ceilings, the auditorium style seating and the perforated walls made the band room unique.

"Just sit anywhere in the back," Ms. Ashbury said before heading back down the hall.

A small group from the beginning band was practicing for a weekend concert. The band instructor, Mr. Hikes, was leading freshman and sophomores like he was maestro of the Boston Pops. In spite of the odds, there were still teachers who actually believed they could make a difference. When he finally noticed me in the back, he motioned for me to come up and sit with the rest of the kids.

"Since you're going to be sitting in here anyway you might as well play something," he said with a shrug, like it wasn't any big deal.

He looked up at the dozens of instruments lining the wall of the band room and then tilted his head and looked back at me. "Clarinet," he said, giving me a wink.

I didn't like that he could take one look at me and presume to know what instrument I could play. But there was something about Mr. Hikes that put me at ease. Everything about him was soft and slow, except for his hands, which seemed to move without him. I suppose a man, as I would find out later, who learned to play five musical instruments without any formal training would have hands that took on a life of their own.

"I always thought that if I did play an instrument, I'd be a flute person," I said as he sat down next to me and opened the clarinet case. He only smiled and then carefully put together the pieces of the clarinet.

"Have you ever played anything before?" he said handing me the clarinet.

Actually, in middle school the music teacher had several instruments she let us play on free days, and the clarinet had been one of them.

"I've played the clarinet, the flute, and the trumpet a few times, just messing around."

He showed me the fingering for C and G, circled the C's and G's on the sheet music and numbered the beats between each of the notes.

Then he told me to jump in and play the C's and G's when we got to them in the song. I thought he was crazy. There was no way I could just start playing when I'd never had any formal training in my life.

"Sit in the middle," a fat kid said. "That way if you mess up it will be harder for anyone to notice."

Hopefully it would be harder for anyone to figure out I was only pretending to play and moving my fingers around on the instrument, I thought as I moved into the middle.

But when everyone started playing, I had the urge to join in. Following the notes the way Mr. Hikes had set it up for me wasn't really that difficult. It was a slow song and there was a pause each time before the clarinets were to come in and play C.

The next song was too difficult for me to play any notes, but there was one other I joined in on before practice was over. Mr. Hikes took the clarinet apart for me and told me I could take it home and practice the notes. He said they were having practice again next week and until then I could think about joining the band.

When Dad picked me up I forgot all about being angry for having to wait so long. All I wanted to know was if I could join the band.

"Sure, sounds good," Dad said without looking at me.

He wasn't even paying attention to what I was saying. I could have asked to join the Fairfield striptease team and he would have said, sure, sounds good, just the same.

I carried that clarinet case like it contained the Hope Diamond. As soon as I got home, I opened the case, making sure I could remember how to put it together. It was ebony black and bright silver, laid to rest in folds of crushed blue velvet. I held it between my hands and stared at it. Maybe it wasn't a diamond, but it was hope.

The next day I dropped one of my classes and switched my schedule around so I could be in band. But they said I'd have to wait until the beginning of the fourth quarter, sometime in the middle of March to start going to the different classes. Mr. Hikes said that would work out better anyway because it would give me a few weeks to practice with just the clarinets and flutes after school before playing with the full band.

Being in the band gave me a newfound confidence I hadn't experienced in months. A few days later I decided to call the Fort Wayne Police Department again.

"I need to talk to the officer who was at my mom's accident when she died," I said, trying to sound professional. But I still had a fourteen-year-old voice.

"You need to call Permanent Records. I can give you their web address."

"Please," I interrupted before she had a chance to spew out the address and then hang up and get back to more important things. "I've been trying to get someone to help me for weeks. I'm always getting the run-around because I'm a kid."

She sighed. "Give me your mom's name and the date of the accident. I'll see what I can find out."

I could tell she wanted to help. But she was probably just a clerk or a receptionist. She didn't have time to search through files and computer records to find an accident report that happened five months ago.

"Thanks," I said, hoping for that one in a thousand chance she might actually do something.

Chapter Seven

That night Abbie made the mistake of making mashed potatoes and fried chicken for dinner. She should have stuck to baking cookies and having picnics on the living room floor. Fried Chicken had been Mom's signature dish, and she also made pretty good mashed potatoes. Abbie's food wasn't awful, but it wasn't nearly as good as Mom's.

No one actually said anything but it was obvious from the looks on our faces and by how slowly we were eating that it wasn't as good as it could have been. The chicken wasn't very juicy and the coating was too salty. And the more I ate of the potatoes, the lumpier they seemed to get.

"You don't like it, do you?" she said in a whiny voice, glaring at Dad.

"Everything is fine," he insisted. "It's just different from what we're used to."

No one said anything about it after that, but when we all dove into dessert -- which was store bought -- Abbie stormed out of the kitchen. Dad got up and went after her. I wanted to believe he only went after her because he didn't want to eat anymore of her food. But I knew he probably had real feelings for her. As far as I was concerned, she was trying to compete with Mom. That was one battle she'd never win.

But the real shocker came a few days later when she came over and brought a little kid with her. She plopped him down on the sofa and started talking to Dad while Joey and I just looked at each other. After a few minutes it was obvious the kid was her son but she didn't even bother to introduce him. She just sat him there between her and Dad like he belonged there as much as Joey and me.

"Hey, Kyle, how are you doing?" Dad said, tickling him in the ribs.

Obviously, Dad had met him before. I wondered what else we'd find out about Abbie out of the blue. I still didn't know much about her except that she worked as a secretary or an assistant of some sort in an office downtown.

After that she started bringing Kyle over more often until it reached the point that he was at our house nearly as much as she was. When she spent the night, she had him sleep on the couch. I was waiting for her to try and shove him into Joey's room. I felt bad for Joey, because that was obviously her next step. I was just glad she didn't have a daughter. Then again, who knew? I was always waiting for the other shoe to drop.

Kyle was only a year younger than Joey but he was small for his age. He wasn't a bad looking kid. He did whine a lot, and worst of all, he was sneaky and manipulative. The night Dad and Abbie ordered pizza he wiped his pizza sauce hands on the sofa, spilled orange soda on the carpet, and then denied it.

"Why don't you take the boys in Joey's room to play," Dad said when we were all done eating. So now they were both lumped in the same category known as "the boys". I sighed and called them into the bedroom and tossed a few of Joey's toys on the floor for them to play with. It didn't take long to find out that this kid was also a pathological liar. He picked a toy truck up off the floor, popped a wheel off and then threw it back down.

"Why did you tear that wheel off?" I said.

"I didn't. It fell off," he said, looking straight at me.

Thankfully, Joey was digging for something under his bed and didn't see that his truck was broken. I snatched the truck and the wheel off the floor and tossed it in the closet before he could see what happened.

The next night Dad and Abbie went out for dinner and left Kyle with us. Dad said he'd give me twenty bucks if I watched both him and Joey. Dad left a bucket of chicken for the three of us to eat.

"I'm still hungry," Kyle said after we'd finished eating and everything was gone.

"Come into the kitchen," I said. "I'll see what we have."

I knew there wouldn't be much. It wasn't like Dad kept the fridge and the cabinets stocked. He rarely went to the grocery. Most of the time we ordered take-out or stopped at convenience stores. I opened the cabinets and Kyle and Joey scanned the shelves.

"You can have microwave popcorn or chicken and noodle soup," I said.

"I see a box of spaghetti and a can of pasta sauce up there," Kyle said. "I want that."

"I'm not taking the time to boil pasta and cook sauce," I told him. "It's either popcorn or soup."

"What's in the fridge?" he demanded.

This kid was really starting to annoy me, but I was afraid if he complained too much when Dad got home, I wouldn't get the twenty bucks.

I opened the fridge. It was even emptier than the cabinets. At least he didn't ask me to open the freezer. We had a frozen cherry pie I was saving for the weekend.

"I'll take the popcorn," Kyle finally said. Joey just nodded his head. He'd eat anything.

"And put extra butter on it," Kyle added as he stomped out of the kitchen.

I tried to make sure the rest of the evening ran as smoothly as possible. I divided the popcorn evenly into two separate bowls and made sure they both had an equal amount of soda poured into cups that were the same size and color.

They still found something to fight about, though I wasn't sure what it was since I was in the kitchen cleaning melted butter out of the microwave when it all started. All I knew was that by the time I got to the living room a food fight had erupted.

"Kyle tried to take some of my popcorn!" Joey yelled.

"You had more than me!" Kyle said, making a weird face.

I glared back at him. "It was divided equally."

"Well, Joey spilled my soda!"

"That's because I was trying to get back the popcorn you stole from me."

When I finally got a chance to look around the room, I saw that popcorn was smashed into the carpet and butter was smeared on the TV screen. Then I saw the soda that had spilled across the coffee table and splattered on the arm of the sofa.

"That's it!" I screamed. "Both of you buttholes into the kitchen to finish whatever is left. And if you start fighting again, I'm coming in there and throwing the rest of it in the trash!"

They didn't fight anymore but it took me almost twenty minutes to clean up the mess in the living room. This wasn't worth twenty bucks.

When Dad and Abbie got home, Kyle was asleep on the sofa.

"Isn't he just a little angel?" Abbie said, stroking his hair. I wanted to throw up, but I had to stay out there and smile long enough to make sure I got my money.

"How did everything go?" Dad said, handing me two tens.

"Fine," I said, grabbing the money. I was tired, the evening was over, and it wasn't worth starting anything now.

Chapter Eight

A few days later Mary Frances did it again! It was at the exact same time during the day that it had happened before. She was walking behind me as I was going past Dani's locker. I was on the other side of the hall, trying to stay hidden in the crowd so Dani wouldn't see me. But Mary Frances had a voice that boomed like a canon. This time she yelled, "Your daddy must have quit while he was making you!"

She had an eerie way of throwing her voice so it sounded like it was coming from me. Dani spun around and we locked eyes. I tried to take off running again but this time I wasn't quick enough. She grabbed me by the neck and swung me around until my feet left the ground. When I finally landed, I was backed up against the lockers and a crowd had gathered in a semi-circle around us. They'd left just enough space for Dani to toss me around like a rag doll.

"Now you gonna die!" she said. Her voice sounded like a growling animal. She reached out to grab me again, her hands like bear claws.

But before she could take hold of me, Mary Frances came flying out from the edge of the crowd, slamming Dani to the floor.

It was like watching a crazy hyena attack a big dumb moose. You wouldn't expect the hyena to win, but Mary Frances was so fast, so brutal, that she beat Dani to a bloody pulp in a matter of seconds. It was almost like watching a cartoon fight. You couldn't see anything but flailing arms and legs and streaks of motion.

I think she might have killed Dani if Mr. Pippens, the science teacher, hadn't stepped in and pulled her back. Mary Frances got hauled to the office and was suspended for three days. The school nurse tried to take Dani to the office to see if she needed any stitches, but she refused to go. She went to the restroom, washed off all the blood and then went to her next class. I suppose she figured the only way she could salvage her reputation was by acting tough after the fact.

During the next few days I found out a lot about Mary Frances. She was an only child who had spent most of her life in New Jersey. Her mom was a former stripper and her dad was a real estate agent. She wouldn't answer to Mary or Frances, only Mary Frances and sometimes not even to that. And supposedly she was gay.

When she came back to school, I sat with her again at lunch. "I'm sorry that you got suspended for three days."

She shrugged. "Not a big deal. I needed a break from this dump anyway."

We both ate greasy sausage pizza and talked for a few minutes about the things she did during her break from Fairfield. Then I finally asked what I really wanted to know.

"Are you gay?" I said.

She smiled. Her tiny, pearly teeth shined like baby corn kernels all in a row. For a second I didn't know if she was going to hit me or burst out laughing.

"No, I like boys," she said, digging into a pile of chocolate pudding that had a crusty film over the top of it. "But I like to keep people guessing."

I nodded. She shoved a spoonful of the pudding into her mouth and I shuddered. The lunches here were disgusting.

"Thanks for taking care of Dani for me," I said.

"I told you I would," she said. "Besides, I've been looking for an excuse to get her for a long time."

It surprised me that Mary Frances thought she needed an excuse. She sopped up the rest of her pudding with the pizza crust and popped it in her mouth. While she was still chewing, she stood up. "By the way, I'm having a party this Friday. You're invited." She licked pudding off her fingers and walked away.

***

That afternoon a guy who said he was from Family and Children's Services showed up at the house. I almost didn't let him in. For all I knew he was a serial killer making up some lame story to get into the house.

"We're not supposed to let anyone in when Dad's gone," I said through the crack in the door.

"Call the downtown office," he said, sliding his card under the door. "They can verify who I am."

I was more scared when I found out he was telling the truth than if he would have been some weirdo trying to mess with a couple of kids. I unlocked the door and let him into the living room. While I'd been making the phone call, I told Joey to pick up all the junk everywhere. Then I told him to go to his room and stay quiet. I had a bad feeling about this.

"My name is Mr. Frank," he said once he was inside. He sat down on the couch and made himself comfortable. He explained that it was procedure for Children's Services to send someone to check on the kids when a parent had died suddenly. He pulled a small pad of paper and a pen out of his shirt pocket, and then asked, "Is your brother here?"

How did he know I had a brother? And he obviously knew Dad was at work because he didn't ask where he was. There was an uncomfortable silence while we were waiting for Joey to come out. But when he sat down on the sofa between us, the caseworker started acting all sweet and sappy toward Joey.

"Hey, Joey, how are you doing? My name is Mr. Frank," he said, patting him on the head like he was the family dog.

I didn't know if Frank was actually his last name or if he wanted us to call him that because he treated all kids like babies in preschool. All my teachers in preschool were called by their first names. I remembered Ms. Tamara and Ms. Susan. The thought of calling him Mr. Frank if that was his first name made me nauseas so I decided not to call him anything.

He started out asking things like how we were doing in school and what our favorite subjects were. Then he asked, "Are you both eating regularly?"

"Sure," I said, making sure to sound offended. "We get all the food we want."

Joey nodded in agreement.

Of course, it was mostly junk food but he didn't ask for specifics. He wrote a few things down on the tablet, but held it back so I couldn't see what he'd written.

He talked about how tough it was to lose a parent and asked if we had ever talked to anyone about our feelings. I told him I'd talked to the priest at Saint Augustine. Joey didn't say anything. I don't think he had ever really talked to anyone.

After that Mr. Frank noticed a small bruise on Joey's arm and asked him how he got it.

Joey shrugged. "I think I fell down on the playground."

Then he asked if Dad ever got mad and hit us. "You can tell me if he has," Mr. Frank said in a soft voice.

But Joey plainly answered no. Dad had never hit either of us, before or after Mom died.

"Do you have any other bruises?" Mr. Frank asked.

"Maybe. I don't know," Joey said, holding out his arms.

Joey's a seven-year-old boy, I thought. Of course, he's going to have bruises. The kid is constantly running and jumping, and only falls down about fifty times a day. He set the pad on his knee and started writing some more.

When there wasn't anything else obvious on Joey to look at, Mr. Frank started looking around the house. After that he stuffed the little pad of paper back in his shirt pocket. "If you need anything give me a call," Mr. Frank said, handing me another business card.

As soon as he left, I threw away the card he gave me as well as the one he'd slid under the door. We never did tell Dad he stopped by.

The next day in gym class I told Tara about Mr. Frank. I figured since she'd been through the system she might know more about why he would come over and if I should expect him back anytime soon.

"A guy from Family and Children's Services came to our house to check on Joey and me yesterday," I said. "He said it was procedure, that they always do that when a parent dies suddenly."

"That's a load of bull," Tara said. "They don't just show up if somebody's Mom dies. Believe me, I know how they operate. Someone called downtown and told them your dad was abusing you or not feeding you or something like that."

"Are you sure?" I said. "The city keeps records of how people die and if they have young kids."

Tara chuckled. "They've got such a heavy caseload that they can barely keep up with all the kids on their list. You think they're just going to stop by out of the goodness of their heart to make sure you're feeling okay?"

She had a point. But who would want to make up things about my dad to get him in trouble? At first, I thought it might be Dorothy Atkins. She always had her nose in everyone's business and thought it was up to her to save the whole world. But then I figured it had to be Abbie. If she could get the bratty kids sent to foster care, she could have Dad all to herself.

Chapter Nine

With everything that was going on in my life, I felt the walls closing in. I was more desperate than ever to find out the truth about how my mother died. It was obvious that the police weren't going to take me seriously and that I'd have to look in another direction. That night after Dad and Abbie had gone out and Joey was asleep, I saw my chance. I went into Dad's bedroom and searched through the dresser drawers, the bathroom, the closet, anyplace where Mom used to keep her things.

In the drawer where she always kept her lotion and make-up, I found the prescription bottle Dad had thrown in my face, along with antacid and an over-the-counter pain reliever. My hands were shaking as I picked up the bottle. Why had he put it back instead of throwing it out? It wasn't like Mom was going to need it anymore.

That's when I got an idea. Near the bottom it did say there was one refill left. I called the number on the bottle.

"Walgreens Pharmacy, how can I help you?" the voice on the other end said.

I took a deep breath to calm my nerves.

"This is Kathy Kimmel," I said, trying to change my voice. "I need to have a prescription refilled."

She asked me for some information and I read it off the bottle. I coughed a little bit each time the pharmacist talked, hoping she'd think I had a cold and that was the reason my voice didn't sound quite like an adult.

"That prescription was canceled. You'll need to see your doctor if you need more."

"Thank you," I said as I turned off the phone. Had the doctor stopped the prescription? Had Mom been better before she died? Or had Mom canceled it herself, knowing she'd never need it again after the end of October, whether she was better or not? Unfortunately, I now had even more unanswered questions than before.

***

Abbie had only been unofficially moved into the house for a few weeks, about the length of time it took a newlywed couple to go on their honeymoon. After that everything between her and Dad started falling apart. Little things she would do that he hadn't seemed to notice before started getting on his nerves.

The way she took it upon herself to decide if we should eat out or stay in or if it would be Italian or Mexican. It was starting to annoy him. Then she would disappear and fade into the background when it was time to pay. She would brag about herself, how thin she was compared to most women, showing off her razor thin body in ridiculous little outfits.

He was constantly telling her not to smoke in the house, especially after the fire, but she did it anyway. He even tried to compromise and said she could smoke in the basement and on the back porch, but she did it everywhere. The whole house stank of Salem Lights. The smell clung to the furniture like the stench of a rotten grill.

But the biggest problem was the money issue. She was constantly asking him for cash. She even had the nerve to ask him to open a joint checking account after finally admitting she had bad credit. I heard them arguing about it one evening after dinner.

"You make decent money," she said while rubbing his back.

I wanted to rip her arm out of its socket.

He hesitated, then made excuses, not having the courage to come out and say no. What did he expect? He'd only known her for a few months. Even I knew better than to allow someone to move into my personal space in such a short time.

But the alcohol seemed to melt his frustration like ice in an August sun. The more he drank, the more he let her get away with. I figured even Dad would have to see through it before too much longer.

That time came sooner than I anticipated. It was after midnight on a school night when voices in the living room woke me up. I was still half asleep when I crawled out of bed and peeked through the crack in my bedroom door. I got there just in time to watch the drama unfold.

"This is all happening too fast," Dad said, waving his hands frantically.

"But I've been taking care of you and the kids," she said, sounding insulted.

Taking care of us? She was smothering Dad, treating Joey like a baby and for the most part ignoring me.

"I know you've really been trying to make things work," Dad said as she rested her fingers on the top of his shoulders.

For a moment I was afraid that she was going to lure him back in. He was a fish caught on the line.

"When I bring Kyle to move in we'll all be a family," she said.

I couldn't believe what I was hearing. The only thing worse than having Abbie here would be that grubby little kid tagging along.

"I don't think Betsy and Joey are ready to have another child living in the house. It's just too soon," Dad said shaking his head.

"Did they say something bad about Kyle?" Abbie said, the tone in her voice rising.

"It's not that," Dad insisted. "This house really isn't big enough for three kids. Kyle would have to share a room with Joey and I don't think it would work out right now."

She quickly folded her arms across her chest. "I thought you liked Kyle. What have you got against my son?"

She wasn't going to let it go. Her usual cool demeanor and calculated manipulations melted under the haze of alcohol and maternal instinct. I was fearful of what would happen next. She had suddenly morphed into a different creature, one with fangs and claws.

"I don't have anything against your son. It's just that, well, the kids say sometimes he takes things from their bedrooms without asking."

She began pacing back and forth, the anger building in her like a volcano. "It was Betsy who accused him of taking things, wasn't it?"

"It doesn't matter," Dad said. "It's just not going to work out for both of you to move in."

"Betsy's a lying brat," she said. Then she used a few more choice words to describe me. As awful as it was to hear her say those things at least I knew those words had slapped my dad out of the emotional coma he'd been in.

"I think you need to leave," he said in a deep voice.

I backed away from the door, thinking the worst was over and she'd finally go away. I was wrong. She'd invested too much time and energy to let it go without rendering some vengeance. That's when I heard screaming and delicate objects crashing against the wall.

I knew I shouldn't have gone back to the door. I should have just crawled in bed and pulled the blanket over my head, but I was drawn like a magnet. When I got back to the crack in the door she was swearing and throwing anything she could get her hands on.

"Your kids never gave me a chance! They ruined everything for us!" she yelled, her eyes as black as a moonless night.

"That's right, they're kids!" Dad retaliated. "You're the one who's supposed to make the effort."

Then she started crying, her last-ditch effort to play on his sympathies. I could see the shattered remains of a vase Grandma Haynes had given us in pieces on the floor.

But her phony tears weren't enough to recast the spell.

"You need to get your things together and leave," he said, barely above a whisper.

"I'm the best thing that happened to you since your wife died," she said with arrogance. "Maybe even before she died, considering she was a mental case."

"Don't say another word about Kathy," he said, his voice shaking. "You could never compare to my wife."

Abbie froze, and for a moment we were all suspended in time. I knew she would explode the moment the shock subsided, but for those few seconds I relished in the truth. My mother was a saint compared to a woman like Abbie, a woman who smoked and swore and paraded through the house in see-through underwear when there was a seven-year-old boy around.

When Abbie finally came to her senses, she let forth her final fury. She lunged at Dad, hitting, kicking and screaming. She had taken him by surprise, and for a second or two it looked like she might get the better of him. But when he finally got his arms around her, he dragged her outside and threw her on the front lawn.

Dad took her things out of the bedroom and bathroom and tossed them out the door, watching as she packed her car. When I finally heard the car start and the screeching of the tires, I collapsed on my bed. Even then I feared it might not be over. I pictured her coming back twenty minutes later with a gun, breaking into the house and shooting us all.

Dad didn't go to bed either. I could hear him pacing back and forth in the living room, occasionally stopping to pick up a piece of glass and throwing it in the trash can. I fell asleep about thirty minutes later to the soft lull of Dad's footsteps.

Chapter Ten

Mary Frances Piccard lived toward the north side of town in a housing addition I never even knew existed. Dad pulled into Rivergreen Drive and I was surprised by how nice the houses were. Large brick homes with immaculate flower gardens and neatly mowed lawns were surrounded by smoothly paved drive-ways and cobblestone sidewalks.

Dad pulled up to the curb and dropped me off at the sidewalk. "Have fun at the party," he said. "Call me when you're ready to come home."

"Sure, Dad," I said. He must have thought I was going to some little kid party with balloons and hats and pin the tail on the donkey. It wasn't that long ago that I'd been doing things like that. He waved as he drove away.

I had no idea what kind of party this would be. But from what I knew about Mary Frances, I didn't think there would be any balloons or shiny hats. The closer I came to the house, the louder the music got. I knocked on the front door, but it didn't surprise me that no one answered. The music was so loud the base was pounding in my head.

I pushed a little and the door opened, so I walked inside. No one even noticed me walking in. People were everywhere. Most were standing or sitting, and a few were lying on the floor. The tables and furniture were littered with beer bottles, soda cans, and bags of potato chips. I felt like Alice falling through the rabbit hole. The prim and proper neighborhood was only an illusion, a mirage to cover up what was really going on inside.

"Hey! Over here!" a girl with red spiked hair yelled when I was half-way across the living room. "Want a taco? We got plenty in the kitchen."

Someone else said there was a taco bar set up in the kitchen. I hadn't eaten much for dinner and tacos sounded good, until I got close enough to see what a mess it all was. It might have been good about two hours ago, before everything got mixed together and what looked like Mountain Dew had been poured into the sour cream. At least I hoped it was Mountain Dew. The only other alternative made me want to throw up.

When two guys came in and started eating out of everything with their hands, I couldn't stand being in the same room with the taco bar anymore.

The red-haired girl came into the kitchen and poured herself a coke. She said most of the kids were either in the finished basement watching music videos or in the living room playing cards. That was why I sat in the dining room where it wasn't nearly as crowded.

I recognized a girl from one of my classes at school and sat next to her. We sat around the elegant dining room table in high backed chairs talking about teachers we didn't like. Then Mary Frances came bolting out of the kitchen with a taco in her hand. Sour cream was dripping everywhere. In the other hand she had a drink in a tall frosty glass with lots of ice cubes.

She stuffed the taco in her mouth and ate it in one bite. Then she pointed a finger at me and smiled. "Hey, glad to see you could make it," she said as sour cream dripped down her chin. She pulled up a chair and sat down at the table with the rest of us.

A skinny boy with bad skin sat at the head of the table. He smiled and pulled a baggie out of his shirt pocket. Inside was what looked like dried leaves. He took a small pipe out of his pants pocket and started stuffing the leaves in the opening at the end.

"Wait until you all get a load of this," he said as he continued to pack the pipe. "It'll blow the top of your head off."

I thought, yeah, just what I need. But everyone else at the table was cheering.

"I think I'll see what's happening in the living room," I said, getting up from the table.

Mary Frances gave me the thumbs up, but the others just ignored me. I guess they were too excited about getting the top of their heads blown off to notice I was leaving.

Apparently, some high school kids who lived in the neighborhood were at the party too. Most of them were in the basement so I decided to try my luck down there. Surprisingly there wasn't anyone getting stoned or drunk in the basement. I sat down next to some kids who were watching music videos and quickly realized that they had already accomplished the task before coming downstairs.

The kid sitting next to me turned his head a couple of times, slapped me in the face with the end of his ponytail and then started laughing hysterically.

"Sorry, man!" he said. He couldn't stop laughing. He thought it was the funniest thing in the world to hit someone in the face with his ponytail.

Then he turned to me and said, "What's your name? I forgot already."

"You didn't forget because I never told you," I said.

He thought that was funny, too.

He reached between his legs and pulled out a beer and took a swig. I didn't even know he had a beer since his sweatshirt had been covering it.

"What is your name?" he said after he finally stopped laughing.

"Betsy," I said.

Then he started laughing again. That was it. I was getting out of here. Before I could get up he grabbed hold of me. He tried to kiss me but was so drunk he missed. He was hanging onto my shirt to steady himself and ended up kissing my shoulder. His mouth and hands were greasy and smelled like Chinese take-out.

"You're so pretty, Betty. Why don't you like me?" he said.

"My name is Betsy, and I don't even know you." I pushed him off me as hard as I could. That was a big mistake. He fell backwards and his beer flew forward, soaking the front of my shirt.

While he was hanging over the back of the sofa, I made my getaway and headed back upstairs. Mary Frances was in the living room when I came bolting up the stairs.

"What happened? Did you pee on yourself?" some kid said, pointing at my shirt.

"It's anatomically impossible for a girl to pee on herself up there," someone else pointed out. At least someone at this party had a few brain cells left.

"You can borrow one of my shirts," Mary Frances said. "My bedroom is upstairs, last one on the left."

I didn't really feel comfortable going upstairs alone and rummaging through the closets but I couldn't go home reeking of Budweiser. The hall was dark and quiet, and I figured no one was up here. Last room on the left, I remembered.

As soon as I flipped on the light switch, I heard a muffled scream. A giggling girl stuck her head out from under the blanket. Her blonde hair was matted and her eyes were bloodshot fire-engine red. It took her a few seconds to focus.

"Look, someone came to join us."

Obviously, there was someone else under there with her, but I couldn't see anyone.

"Don't mind me," I said, trying to act cool. I hurried to the closet and pulled out a shirt.

"Does this make me look fat?" I said, holding it up against myself.

The blonde howled with laughter and dove back under the covers.

All of this made me think of Lydia Greenwald, the "bad" girl at my old middle school. Every school had a few, even the private Catholic ones. Lydia was always defying the dress code with low cut shirts and high heels. She smoked cigarettes under the bleachers during the basketball games and it was rumored that she lost her virginity when she was twelve. But even Lydia paled in comparison to what some of these kids did.

After changing in the bathroom, I walked past what looked like the master bedroom. The door was slightly open and the light was on. I figured there couldn't be anything any worse going on in there than in the last bedroom. It was like being on a game show and trying to decide if I should choose door number one, number two, or number three.

I had better luck this time. There were three guys sitting on the floor playing Black Jack. One was dealing while the other two were sitting across from him.

"Sit down, we're playing for quarters," one of them said.

These three looked interesting enough to be fun, but not as dangerous as the guy who fell down on top of me and spilled beer down the front of my shirt. The dealer said his name was Misha. His accent was heavy, probably eastern European. He had skin as pale as the sky and dark, wavy hair.

After a couple of hands, we started talking about other things besides the card game. Misha talked about how much better real Russian vodka was than the stuff they were serving at this party. The kid sitting next to me started talking about Mary Frances.

"So, is the girl gay or not?" he said, stuffing another quarter into his pocket.

"That's what they say," Misha said. He shuffled the cards and started to deal again.

"Wouldn't surprise me," the other guy said. He slammed the floor with his fist when Misha dealt him a two.

"What do you think?" the kid said looking at me.

"Mary Frances is whatever she feels like at the moment," I said.

After an hour of Black Jack I was ready to go home. The only person I felt comfortable talking with was Misha, and after losing five dollars he left the party. I walked back to the kitchen where it was quieter and called Dad.

A girl who was in my English class must have seen the look on my face after I heard the phone ring at home about twenty times and still no one had answered.

"Is everything okay?" she asked.

"I guess," I said, trying not to act too concerned. "My dad is supposed to be home but he's not answering his phone."

"My sister is picking me up in a little bit. We can take you home," she said. "You live in town, don't you?"

"Yeah," I said, almost laughing. Mary Frances was interesting but I didn't think she was that big of a deal that kids from out of town would come to her party.

The girl said her name was Vivica and that she'd let me know when it was time to go. A little bit turned into an hour and a half, but what could I do? When Vivica's sister finally showed up with her boyfriend I realized it might not be so smart to leave with people I barely knew. But Dad still wasn't answering and Vivica seemed to be one of the more rational people I'd been around tonight.

It was almost twelve by the time I got home. I was terrified of facing Dad. I'd never been allowed to stay out past eleven.

"Thanks for taking me home," I said, climbing out of the car.

"Sure. See you at school next week," Vivica said.

They'd already driven away by the time I got out my key and opened the door. I was glad they were already gone. I didn't want Dad looking out the window and asking a million questions about who brought me home.

But Dad was snoring, passed out, stone cold drunk on the sofa. The living room smelled like sour wine mingled with the stench of a man who hadn't showered in several days. I was angry that I'd been so worried about getting in trouble.

After checking on Joey, I went to my bedroom and shut the door. I didn't bother putting a blanket on Dad, turning off the television or anything.

Not long after I changed clothes and crawled into bed, Vivica texted me. She just wanted to make sure everyone was alive and breathing at my house and that my kid brother hadn't ran away. It was obvious she was trying to be funny, but underneath the sarcasm I could tell that she actually cared. I texted her back and told her that everything was okay and thanked her again for bringing me home.

I crawled into bed and pulled the covers up to my chin. At least going to the party hadn't been a total waste. The possibility of finding a real friend had finally emerged.

Chapter Eleven

When I was finally able to start my new schedule and play with the entire band, I was shocked to see who was in the third row, fifth seat, playing the saxophone -- Misha. He was the guy I played Blackjack with at Mary Frances' party.

"You never told me you were in the band," I said.

He shrugged. "You never asked. Besides, I don't like to brag."

I thought that was a strange thing to say. Why would anyone think it was bragging to admit you were in the high school band. Then I heard him play. There were four saxophone players in the band, but Misha dominated every note.

After hearing him play he seemed to look different. What had been shaggy, unkempt hair was now sexy, tousled and blowing gently in the dirty air from the overhead air duct.

What had been a bratty teenage smirk was now an interesting, artistic smile. Knowing something important about someone changed your entire perspective of who they were.

When it came to knowing someone and the perception of who they were, I didn't think my understanding of who Tara was could get more complicated -- until the following Tuesday afternoon.

It was the third week in March, a dreary Friday with a steady stream of showers that kept all the gym classes inside. I first noticed that something unusual was going on when the gym teacher was talking on her cell phone. She never did that during class. Then she walked out of the gym and into the hall, going back and forth several times.

When the plain clothes security officer who monitored the halls stepped into the gym while talking on his two-way radio, I knew someone was in serious trouble. No one was doing the warm-ups anymore. Everyone had stopped and was looking around at everyone else, wondering who was going to get called down to the office -- or worse.

We all looked at the usual suspects, the same few kids who always got in the worst trouble. In this particular class that was Josh Kessler, Tabitha Smith, and the fat kid with the long German name no one could pronounce. You could usually tell who was in trouble by the expression on their face or their body language. But none of those kids gave away any of the tell-tale signs. Whoever was in trouble knew how to put on a good show. That's when I looked at Tara. But she didn't flinch, didn't even bat an eye.

She stood still as stone, until the security officer started walking toward her. That's when everything started to happen at once. It was almost like some late night drama you'd see on TV. Without warning, Tara took off like a rocket for the locker rooms.

The police must have already been in the building because they were inside the gym in a matter of seconds, cornering Tara before she got past the bleachers. She started to fight, but one of the officers flipped out a pair of handcuffs and had her hands locked behind her back before she could do much damage.

"You like bruising and breaking the arms of kids!" she screamed.

The officers didn't even respond. At first I thought it was ridiculous that they had to do this in the middle of class in front of all the kids. But after I thought about it, I realized that if they had called her down to the office over the intercom it would have just given her more time to run away. They must have known who they were dealing with. They basically drug her out of the gym kicking and screaming.

I started thinking about all the people who got into serious trouble in this school and how Tara was so different from most of the others. Dani was brutal, primal; you could see an enemy like that coming a mile away. She'd get arrested for selling drugs or beating up someone's grandma, not anything too complicated. Dani wasn't smart enough to be truly evil.

I figured Tara was capable of something like gas lighting an old lady or slowly poisoning someone, which made imagining what she got arrested for that much more interesting.

When I got home that afternoon I still couldn't stop thinking about what happened to Tara. I kept looking over at the Atkins house, wondering what was going on inside. I figured if it was serious enough to drag her out of school in handcuffs that she probably wouldn't be back there anytime soon.

But every ten or fifteen minutes I kept looking over there, thinking I'd see a police car, or a vehicle from Family and Children's Services. Instead, after looking out the window at least five times, I saw a car pulling up toward our house.

I opened the door and was shocked to see Mrs. Craig, the secretary from Saint Augustine. She was standing on our front porch holding a large box.

"Hi Betsy," she said, peeking around the box. "I have some things that you left at school."

It must not have been anything too important because I didn't even realize I was missing anything. I almost told her, thanks, but you can either donate it or throw it out. But then I remembered that Mrs. Craig had been friends with Mom. It wasn't like they'd been best friends or anything, but they did some fundraisers together at church and had known each other for years. This was my chance to get some information.

"Come in," I said.

She sat down on the sofa, with the big box on her lap.

"You can just set that down anywhere," I said, uninterested at the prospect of what was in the box. But there were things in the box I hadn't anticipated.

"I had to walk home from the church one day and I'd forgotten my hat and gloves and your mom let me borrow these," Mrs. Craig said, carefully pulling out the items.

It was a hand crocheted scarf and matching mittens in blue and green, Mom's favorite colors. She looked like she regretted saying it, but it was the perfect opening.

"So you knew my mom pretty well?" I said.

She slowly nodded, like she had to think about it for a moment. Then she said, "Fairly well. We went to the same high school, so I knew her a little better back then."

"Were you and Mom in any activities together in school?" I asked.

She gave me a strange look, like it was weird for a kid to be asking something like that at this point. But I had to start the conversation somewhere.

"We were in the choir together," she said, making it sound like it was no big deal. But I felt a pang in my stomach when she said it. I'd never known Mom was in the choir and I now realized that may have been where I'd gotten my musical inclinations.

"Was my mom ever moody or depressed when she was younger? Was she ever like that around you?" I asked. I realized I'd probably shifted the conversation too soon.

Mrs. Craig looked at me like I was asking about my mom's sex life or something.

I'd changed a lot in the last few months. I wasn't nearly as afraid of things as I was before. I needed answers and didn't have time to be polite.

"Have you asked your dad about this?" she said.

"Yeah, and he said she was. But I need to hear it from someone else before I really believe it."

She looked uncomfortable and I could tell she was ready to make up an excuse to leave so she could get away. I placed my hand on top of hers and asked again. It was shameless, I know. I had to tell her enough of what Dad had said to let her know what was going on, but not too much that it would make Dad look bad. "I'm just wondering what she was like when she was younger. He said she'd struggled with depression for a while, and it's not like I can ask her anymore."

She pretended to be looking in the box for something as she gathered her thoughts.

"Sometimes your mom was moody," she said with a nervous smile. "Then again, aren't most teenage girls?"

I didn't want to stop the flow of information so I just shook my head in agreement. "So, what do you mean by moody?" I asked, thinking how clever I was to string her along. But she took off on a tangent after that, babbling on about her and Mom and some ex-boyfriend Mom couldn't decide if she really liked or not.

When she started looking at her watch, I realized I wasn't as clever as I thought.

"I probably should be going," she said.

"Thanks for bringing over this stuff," I said, getting up and following her to the door.

After she left, I looked through the box. There were folders, a few books, and a hat I had left at school. The box was barely half full. The fact that there was so little left after my time at Saint Augustine bothered me. I closed the box and set it in the basement along with a pile of other old things we were planning on throwing out.

Chapter Twelve

Something in me had changed somewhere between the incident with Abbie and the night of Mary Frances's party. Maybe it had been happening for several months and I hadn't noticed until now. Maybe it would have happened even if Mom wouldn't have died. No matter how it occurred, I had become someone I never thought I'd be. The way I dressed was different. The way I talked and laughed had changed. The way I thought and looked at the world had morphed into something I'd never experienced before.

I decided to change my name to match my new personality. Since my full name was Elizabeth, I decided the easiest thing to do was to come up with another shortened version besides Betsy. Liza seemed to suit me much better now.

The problem was telling Dad. I wasn't sure what the best approach was. Since he'd told me about Mom's depression and that she possibly committed suicide, we rarely talked about anything anymore. It was weird that he'd drop a bomb like that and then we'd never discuss it again. Then again, what else was there really left to say?

The day he told me he'd been called to Fairfield to discuss my grades turned out to be a good time to bring up the name change.

"Your grades have slipped," he said while flipping through sheets of paper the guidance counselor had given him. "I know the work isn't any harder at this school, and they even use some of the same textbooks," he said. "Are the teachers explaining things?"

He was grasping at straws, trying to figure out any explanation for why I was sinking without putting the blame where it really belonged -- on me. I only did what I had to do to get by. The work was boring and I figured as long as I passed, compared to most everyone else at this school, I was ahead of the curve.

"Your homeroom teacher says you're rude in class, even defiant," Dad said, moving on to what we both really wanted to talk about.

"Mr. Cooper?" I said, rolling my eyes. "I'm only in there twenty minutes in the morning. We don't even do real work there."

"He says you sign in every morning as Liza Kimmel. He says you won't even answer to Betsy anymore."

"None of the other teachers said anything about it, did they?"

Dad narrowed his eyes. "You've been using the name Liza in all of your classes."

"Betsy is such a baby name," I said, trying to get him to feel sorry for me.

"But your mom called you Betsy. She loved that name," he said, turning the tables on me, almost choking out the words.

But something in me snapped and I didn't care if he started crying or not. "You're right. *Mom* called me Betsy, and she's gone now. Sweet, little Betsy left the day she did."

Dad just stared at me for a second. Then he slowly nodded his head. "So, you want to be called Liza now." He couldn't look at me when he said it.

"There are worse things I could be doing than changing my name," I said. "Besides, there are a lot of nicknames for Elizabeth and Liza is one of them."

"I guess," he said. Then he mumbled, "You weren't like this at Saint Augustine, even after your mom died."

I almost laughed out loud. "I'm not at Saint Augustine anymore. Fairfield is completely different."

He wasn't arguing back anymore. He just got up and walked out of the kitchen.

I thought how comparing Fairfield to Saint Augustine was like comparing Wal-Mart to Saks Fifth Avenue or Motel 6 to the downtown Hilton. The food was different. The people were different. Even the air smelled different. At Saint Augustine the halls smelled like dried flowers and the office like the principal's aftershave. It wasn't that Fairfield smelled bad, just fake. The custodians were always sterilizing everything and spraying chemicals and cleaners everywhere.

I went to my bedroom and blasted the radio. I knew I hadn't exactly been right about sweet little Betsy leaving the day Mom died.

She tried to stick around, she really did. But she hadn't left all at once. She had drifted away like smoke, with each shift of the wind taking fragments and pieces. Betsy left one bit at a time until nothing was left.

A few days after Dad agreed that I could be called Liza, Joey came home insisting he wanted to change his name, too.

"I want to be called Antonio," he said, trying to talk with an Italian accent.

I started laughing. He sounded ridiculous.

"It's not any dumber than you being Liza," he said.

"My full name happens to be Elizabeth," I said. "At least Liza is a nickname for Elizabeth. Antonio has nothing to do with David Joseph."

I knew he didn't want to be called Davy. A kid in our neighborhood he couldn't stand was named Davy. That didn't leave many options.

After Joey thought about it he started to cry, and when Dad heard about it he said he'd had enough. "No more name changes in this house," he said.

Joey didn't speak to me for two days because I got to keep Liza and he couldn't be Antonio. Two days is a long time for a little kid. But I figured out that it really didn't matter if I got to change my name or not, at least not at home.

None of us ever called each other by our first names anyway. The three of us rarely used our names at all, unless we were yelling for someone from one side of the house to the other. Mom was the only one who had acknowledged our individuality or took pleasure in calling each of us by name. We weren't quite as real now that she was gone. Our status as human beings had diminished in her absence.

***

That weekend Vivica and I made plans to meet at the mall. Dad dropped me off Friday at six.

"Pick me up at midnight," I said.

He gave me a strange look. "The mall closes at ten. I'll be back then."

"But the movie theater is open until midnight," I said quickly.

"You're not going to the movies. I'll be back at ten." He drove away before I could say anything else. When he was relatively sober it was difficult to argue with him, or at least confuse him enough to get my way.

Vivica was waiting at the food court like we'd planned. "Let's go to Windsor and try on dresses," she said, motioning for me to follow her. "We can come back and eat later."

Even though I'd filled out quite a bit in the last few months, Vivica was the one who really looked good in a slinky dress. But she didn't make me feel bad about it. She told me which dresses complimented my figure and which ones I looked bad in.

"Let's go to the Asian Hutch," she said after we had tried on several dresses and the sales clerk started giving us the evil eye. "The website showed these really cool shirts from India they just got in."

Certain colors like beige and yellow washed me out, but once again, Vivica looked good in everything. She reminded me of one of those Hollywood starlets you'd see on the tabloid TV shows, with yellow blonde hair and heavy eyelids full of regret. Her life was complicated, and had sometimes even been disastrous, but she always looked good no matter what was going on. And she smiled and laughed a lot.

"You never get down about anything," I said.

She laughed. "Oh, yeah I do."

"You always seem to be in a good mood when I'm around."

"When my mom left, I thought about killing myself," she said without emotion.

"Glad to see you didn't," was a dumb thing to say but all I could think of at the moment.

We decided we wanted something sweet and headed for the food court.

"I didn't do it, not because I didn't want to, but because I knew I'd botch it."

I almost said, how tough could it be to kill yourself if you really wanted to die? But I didn't want to give her any ideas.

"You mean you were afraid you'd live instead of die?" I said.

She nodded. "I'd probably end up in a coma or paralyzed. I've heard of that happening to kids after they tried to shoot themselves or overdose on drugs."

This conversation made me feel awkward and I glanced down at my watch, pretending to care what time it was.

"If your dad doesn't show up, I can take you home again."

I chuckled. "Is your sister's boyfriend picking you up?"

"No, they broke up. But my dad has a new girlfriend and she's picking me up."

Vivica's dad seemed at ease being a single parent and she didn't seem to mind that a slew of women came in and out of his life. Somehow it seemed to work for them. Or maybe they just didn't care if it worked or not. From what she'd told me, I don't think she ever had a stable home life, even when her mom had still been around. How could you miss something you never had?

We both ordered monster cinnamon rolls smothered in cream cheese icing. Then we laughed how each roll had about a million calories.

"At school you're always eating things like fruit and yogurt when there's pizza and fries," I said. "How come?"

"It's the only place I can get a decent meal on the federal dime," she said, licking cinnamon off her fingers.

I suddenly felt guilty for using Dad's money to buy pizza, burgers and Mexican burritos when Vivica was trying to figure out how to get her next serving of fruits and vegetables.

As the sugar and saturated fat entered our bloodstream we didn't talk for several minutes. I suddenly realized how much I admired Vivica. She was the strongest person I'd ever met. She wasn't strong in the way Dani or Mary Frances was, able to beat someone senseless with their bare hands or intimidate with a stare. Vivica's strength wasn't about destroying someone else, but saving herself.

If you would have dropped Mary Frances, Dani, and Vivica on a deserted island and came back a year later, Vivica would have been the only one still alive. Dani and Mary Frances would have killed each other the first week while Vivica would have been living on the other side of the island, swimming in the lagoon, eating wild berries, and weaving a raft out of bamboo.

Chapter Thirteen

The band class had an interesting group of kids. Eliana, who played trombone, was here illegally from Mexico. Her dad had been deported during an ICE raid. The family had snuck him back over the border in the trunk of a car, only to have him deported again two weeks later. Jason's aunt was folding laundry on the back porch one day when she walked out the door and they never saw her again. The best flute player, Kimberly Stark, had eleven brothers and sisters. There was Misha, of course, and then me. It was amazing how much at home I felt with this motley crew of musicians.

By late March I'd gotten halfway decent on the clarinet. Hr. Hikes told me I had a talent for music. He said some kids connected to the music and the notes flowed from their brains through their fingers without interruption. With most kids, the notes got clogged up somewhere in the process and never came out right. But I'd lost so much of myself during the last several months that it felt like I was hollow inside. Most anything could have flowed through me on an open and clear path. I must have been getting pretty good because Mr. Hikes asked me to participate in the spring recital.

A few weeks before the program the practices became more intense. Forty hormonal bodies shoved into one room without air conditioning was hot and uncomfortable. Some of the kids even got claustrophobic and started breathing heavy. Not me. I liked being crammed in with all of them. I felt safe, like a bug wrapped in a cocoon.

Amelia Filler, however, was overweight and started sweating profusely when the temperature was over sixty degrees in a room. After we played the same song four times in a row, she had a panic attack. She ran out of the room flapping her arms like a bird ready to take off over the woodwind section. She came back in after Mr. Hikes opened a few of the windows and turned on a fan.

After that, Mr. Hikes gave us all a fifteen-minute break. We were supposed to drink water to keep our mouths moist, and stay away from salty snacks. But most of the kids had sodas, candy bars and chips. But not Misha. He was serious about his playing. He drank bottled water and brought in fruit to snack on.

In spite of eating the right things and drinking pricey bottled water, I happened to know that he smoked weed, at least occasionally. If he was really serious about playing, I thought it was ridiculous for him to do that.

"Marijuana smoke is worse for your breathing than cigarettes," I said, trying to make it sound jokey and not judgmental. "By the time you're in college you won't be able to hold the long notes."

"I'm not going to college," he said with a grin. "Actually, I haven't even decided on finishing high school yet. Besides, I can make a living playing the short notes."

I laughed, even though I knew he was probably serious about not finishing high school. Misha could put a spin on almost anything, making himself look good no matter what he did.

Band practice ended that day at five. Since Dad wouldn't pick me up until at least five-thirty, I sat in the commons with the rest of the kids who were waiting on rides. The lunches were so gross that I was usually starving by this time each day. I tore open a Milky Way and ate half of it in two bites. It was so good. I could almost feel the sugar surging through my body. After that I shoved handfuls of corn chips in my mouth and washed it all down with a Mountain Dew.

By five-thirty Misha and I were the only ones waiting for someone to pick us up. As the sinking sun made shadows and shapes dance across the dirty tile floor we talked about teachers, classes, and all the other kids. The second there was a pause in the conversation he leaned over and kissed me.

"You're pretty," he said in a quiet voice. Then he leaned over again, turning this into a full-fledged, awkward make-out session. Other than a few short kisses, I'd never done anything else with a guy. But as much as I'm bumbling through all this, all I can think of is that I'm sure I have sewer breath. My breath must have been awful after a

Milky Way, corn chips, and a Mountain Dew.

I didn't have time to prepare for this with peppermint gum and Binaca Breath Spray.

Misha, however, didn't seem to mind. After we stopped, he had a dreamy look on his face.

Then I looked up and saw Dad parked out front.

"My dad's here. I've got to go."

He nodded the slow, cool guy nod as I got up and slung my backpack over my shoulder.

"Hey," he said, as I was walking away. "Give me your number."

We quickly typed each other's number into our phones before I headed outside. Even though a cold wind tried to blow me over as soon as I walked out the front door, I could still feel the warmth of Misha's body against mine.

But I didn't have long to linger in the moment. Dad started yelling at me before I even had a chance to shut the car door. "What were you doing with that guy! He was practically laying on top of you!"

I didn't even know he'd been able to see inside. "He wasn't laying on top of me. We were just kissing."

"You're only fourteen."

"I am in high school. I can kiss a guy."

"Not like that. I have to start worrying about garbage like this now?" he said. He hit the gas and screeched out of the parking lot.

I almost said something like, this is what you get for sending me to this crappy school. But then he blurted out, "Maybe being in the band isn't such a good idea."

"We were just kissing. Nothing else is happened."

He didn't say anything the rest of the way home, but I could feel the chill of the Red Sea closing in behind me. He just couldn't take being in the band away from me. Right now, it was the only thing carrying me through to the other side.

***

The snow in late March was so sloppy and sloshy that I could hear the wet mess in the driveway splashing against the tires before the car was even up to the house. But this car was squeaking and squealing even more than usual, indicating that the driver was angry and in a hurry. When I peeked through the curtains and saw Grandma Haynes practically jumping out of the car and slamming the door so hard I was certain the glass would crack in two, I dreaded whatever she was here for. The knock on the front door was firm, precise, and in rhythm, just like the clickety-click of her high heels.

"Is your dad here?" she asked as soon as I opened the door.

"No," I said, thinking how fun it would be to push her into a snow drift.

"Good." She stepped around me and stomped into the living room. "I need to talk to you." She sat down and motioned for me to come over, just like she did the day she told me to snap out of it, get a life, and stop moping around because my mom was dead.

"I saw Mrs. Craig yesterday at church," she said without blinking.

Mrs. Craig? It had been a few weeks since she'd stopped by and it took a couple seconds for my mind to backtrack and figure out what this was all about.

"Please don't be telling people your mother was depressed or moody," she said stiffly.

"Your mother is gone. We don't need to start spreading rumors about her."

"Mrs. Craig came over here," I said, making it sound like it was all her fault that I'd even said anything. "She'd been friends with Mom. I just wanted to ask her some things I'd been wondering about."

"If you need to know anything about your mother, ask me," she said stiffly. "I'm the one who raised her and knew her better than anyone."

She wouldn't even acknowledge that Dad existed, let alone that he'd been married to Mom for almost sixteen years.

"Okay, did Mom suffer from depression, would she have ever done anything….to hurt herself?" I said, skipping around the word suicide.

Grandma didn't flinch, but her eyes looked as if they could set a fire. "Of course not. Who told you such a thing."

"I found an old prescription bottle for Mom. It was for anxiety and depression."

She cleared her throat. "That was because she was stressed out. She had to take care of you kids and the house, and hold down a job."

Another not so subtle dig at Dad that Mom had to work, even though it was only part time and she seemed to enjoy her job.

"Your mother was neither depressed nor anxious, simply overworked."

Even though I'd never believe Mom committed suicide without hard facts, Grandma denying it wouldn't convince me of anything. She would deny anything negative about Mom. She couldn't even admit that Mom had been depressed, and that much I knew was true because of the prescription. There was no need to even bring up a possible suicide.

"Now," she said, her voice softening as she took hold of my hand. "There's no need to ever bring this up again with anyone we know, right?"

I nodded eagerly. Of course, there was no need to talk to anyone I knew, they would only lie or deny. No need to say two words to that stupid Mrs. Craig ever again. Total strangers, however, was another matter. But Grandma didn't need to know that. She was the only relative who kept in touch with us and I didn't want to totally alienate her. Who knew when we might need her help. Grandma actually doing something useful for us instead of just complaining about everything happened sooner than I thought.

Chapter Fourteen

Grandma spent more time with me after our conversation about Mom, especially when Dad wasn't around. I wasn't sure if she was really making an effort to be helpful or just keeping an eye on me and making sure I didn't say anything about Mom that would sully the family name.

On Thursday afternoon a car pulled up to the house that neither I nor Grandma recognized. But the second the driver stepped out, a wave of fear jolted through my brain.

"Who's that?" Grandma asked, looking through the front window.

"Abbie, Dad's ex-girlfriend," I said. "I can't believe she has the nerve to come back here after Dad kicked her out in the middle of the night."

The way Grandma glared at Abbie I thought she'd melt a hole through the front window.

That's when I saw my chance to divert the old woman's anger from me onto a more worthy target.

"The night he kicked her out she threw the vase you got Mom for Christmas against the wall and it shattered into a million pieces."

Grandma had her hand on my shoulder and I could feel her fingertips dig in, but she didn't say a word. She pressed the creased out of her skirt, tilted her head back and marched toward the front door. Abbie didn't stand a chance.

I stood a few feet away from the door so Abbie couldn't see me, but I could still hear what they were saying.

"Yes," Grandma said stiffly as soon as she opened the door.

"I'm a friend of Eric's," Abbie said. She was using her sweet, sappy voice. I wasn't sure if she even knew who Grandma was, but I was certain she thought she could easily manipulate some old woman. "Is he here?"

"No," Grandma said. And then she just stood there.

"I'm here to get a silver bracelet I left. I'll come back when Eric is home."

"I'm afraid you're not welcome in this house any longer," Grandma said.

"That bracelet is mine. I have a right to it," Abbie insisted.

"We'll deduct it from the price of the antique vase you destroyed and I'll send you a bill for the remaining amount you owe us," Grandma said.

"Just forget it," Abbie snarled.

The last thing Grandma said was, "And don't ever come back to this house again or we will have you arrested."

I almost started cheering as Grandma slammed the door. As overbearing as Grandma could be, I was glad she was around. I needed her strength when everyone and everything around me was crumbling.

***

Less than a week after the Abbie-Grandma incident, I woke up and realized it was Easter Sunday. I was hoping for an Easter basket, or at least some chocolate bunnies and a few marshmallow peeps. I should have known better.

When I got to the kitchen, Dad was sitting at the table reading the paper. A few minutes later Joey ran out of his bedroom, looking under the chair, and glancing back out into the living room. Dad put the paper down and shook his head.

"There's nothing to look for," he said flatly.

He muttered an apology for not getting Easter baskets put together. I was disappointed but not shocked. After that he said, "Get dressed. We're going to church." And then I was shocked. Dad had dropped Joey and me off at church a few times since Mom died, but I don't think he'd gone at all.

We only had about fifteen minutes to get ready, but I had an Easter outfit from last year and it didn't take me long to get dressed.

Joey, as usual, was difficult. Thank goodness for clip on ties and the fact that Dad had recently had Joey's hair cut so it didn't need brushed to look halfway decent.

Once we got to the church, Dad sat toward the back, but I was by the aisle and had a good view. All the children in the lower Sunday school classes walked down the center aisle of the sanctuary, marching toward the front of the church like little cherubs flocking around the throne of God. The little boys in stiff blue suits and the little girls in pink and white frilly dresses like tiny beauty contestants, all gathered around Father Henderson as he opened his long, frail arms and beckoned them to him.

"Our Littlest Angels Choir will be performing in our service this morning," he said.

I'd almost forgotten how they sounded, their tiny voices all in unison like a cartoon. The littlest ones would make faces, push the kids next to them, and wave to their parents.

After the musical performance, Father Henderson gave a brief sermon. It was the usual Easter sermon; the agony of the cross, the painful separation of the Father and the Son, and the glory of the Resurrection on Easter morning. He had pretty much given the same sermon every year for as long as I could remember. But this year I paid more attention when he talked about how eventually we would all face death, be separated from loved ones, and because of the Resurrection we could look forward to being reunited again.

I clung to those words as if they were the last drops of oxygen in an airless universe. It was amazing how things you'd been taught your whole life could so quickly vanish from conscious thought if you weren't exposed to them on a regular basis. Words like the Trinity, the Synoptic Gospels, and sound doctrine, it all sounded like a language I'd forgotten how to speak.

After the service we all got in the car and Dad started driving. I didn't even know we weren't going home until Dad turned in the opposite direction. Maybe we were going out to eat, but I didn't think there were any restaurants this way. Maybe he was going to visit a friend, but he didn't have any friends he got together with anymore. I was about to ask where we were going when I saw the cemetery.

"Are we going to see Mom's grave?" Joey asked.

Dad nodded and I felt a knot in the pit of my stomach. I suddenly felt lost and small in a cemetery that held nearly a thousand gravesites, the peaked granite and marble headstones pointing toward the heavens. He drove slow, taking his time while heading toward the section where Mom was buried. It was almost like he was preparing himself for the visit. He probably thought he could feel closer to her if he went to church. And when he didn't find her there, I guess he figured this was the next logical place. I had a feeling he'd be disappointed all over again.

He parked the car as close as possible, about thirty yards back from the headstone. He didn't say a word. He didn't tell us to go, to stay, anything. Joey got out of the car when Dad did and walked beside him to the grave. I hesitated, purposely lagging behind. It was the first time I'd been here since the funeral and I wanted to be alone.

I stayed far enough back that I couldn't even read the words on the headstone. My heart was racing and my legs wouldn't carry me any closer. Even if she had committed suicide, it was the depression, the disease that had done it, not the heart and soul of who Mom really was. Since I'd probably never know what really happened, I'd have to come up with my own scenario, a plausible explanation I could convince myself was true -- something reasonable I could live with.

I pretended I was alone, ignoring the two strangers ahead of me, the man and his little boy. When Dad started yelling at the headstone and crying uncontrollably even Joey backed away. I turned around and walked back to the car. I wasn't pretending anymore. I really didn't know him.

Things went downhill for Dad after that day. He started drinking even more, and didn't even try to hide it. He'd walk around the house swigging from an open bottle. On the weekends he'd lay in bed all day, and every few days he'd call in sick to work.

I finally decided I couldn't worry about Dad anymore. What could I do anyway? He was the adult and I was the kid. It wasn't like I could ground him or take away his TV privileges. I had to worry about myself now.

Chapter Fifteen

Almost every weekend someone at Fairfield had a party. The week after spring break Luke Kessler and Jacob Hoffman were having a party at Jacob's brother's house. They were both in my homeroom and Jacob basically invited everyone who sat close to him.

I knew both of these guys were bad news but I hated not having anything to do on the weekends. None of the nice kids ever asked me to do anything. The kids who usually didn't get into any trouble or go out drinking or drugging didn't pay much attention to me. Even though I didn't drink or do drugs, by striking up a friendship with Mary Frances and having Misha as my unofficial boyfriend, I had lumped myself into that category by default. I was thankful I'd found a friend as nice as Vivica.

I found out that Jacob lived less than a mile from our house and I could walk most of the way through the neighborhoods. There was a quarter moon out that night, a chunk of shiny silver in an ebony sky. It was a warm evening in April when I walked across the Martin's back yard. The rising moon was shining between baby leaves and cutting geometric shapes over the lawn. There was enough light that I could easily make my way through the neighbors' yards, but dark enough that if I stayed under the trees, I could remain hidden under the tiny buds of fresh spring leaves.

I figured there'd have to be at least some kids at the party who weren't making out in the bedrooms or getting stoned at the dining room table. I was wrong. This party was even bigger and wilder than the one Mary Frances had. Not only was the inside of the house full, but kids were spilling out into the drive, the front lawn, and into the street.

Supposedly Mary Frances and Vivica were both at the party, but I never found either one of them. After about ten minutes I saw Misha next to a big screen TV. We were in the living room pressed up against crowds of people. I think he asked how it was going with the clarinet, but I could barely hear him. This really wasn't my idea of a good time.

"I probably should be going soon," I said.

"Don't go yet," Misha said. "They're starting a bonfire in the back yard in a few minutes. Will you stay for that?"

"Sure," I said. I was suffocating in this house full of sweaty bodies and marijuana fumes. Going outside sounded good.

We went to the back yard where some older boys were piling sticks into a large stack.

"We're having a burning ceremony," one kid said.

Inside the burn pit was a growing stack of T-shirts, photographs, letters, and other remnants of bad memories, abusive childhoods, and relationships gone wrong. The kid pulled a small bottle of whiskey out of his coat pocket. He laughed while he poured the golden-brown liquid over the stack of ugly mementos. Then he took a swig from the bottle and poured on some more.

The other kid held up a book of matches. "May every evil thought, bad memory, and emotional bondage die in this burn pit," he proclaimed. He struck a match alongside his boot and a bright orange flame instantly erupted. When the match hit the whiskey-soaked pile it exploded like a small bomb.

Kids were clapping and cheering as the flames flickered and danced in the crisp night air. The motion of the fire was almost hypnotic, and along with the increasing warmth, I was lulled into a calm, soothing state. I leaned my head against Misha's shoulder. I was so relaxed that if we would have sat down, I'm sure I would have drifted off to sleep. I closed my eyes for a second, and when I opened them the fire seemed to change and a strange light was reflecting off the trees. What I thought was a strobe light someone had hung up on the porch turned out to be lights from four police cars out front in the street.

"Cops!" somebody yelled.

Suddenly, it turned into a stampede with people screaming and running everywhere. I wasn't a very fast runner and was moving in slow motion compared to the others. I was going to be the one to get caught and hauled downtown to the juvenile holding tank. Misha grabbed hold of my hand and started pulling me along.

"I don't have any experience running away from parties that are getting busted by the cops," I said.

"You're not a good runner, are you?" he yelled back at me.

"I was always a better swimmer than runner," I said.

"If we have a party at the lake, you'll be set."

The way he said it was funny but I was breathing too hard to laugh. It seemed like we'd been running for miles but we were only a few blocks from the party when we stopped. We were squatting down, hiding behind someone's hedge. Misha pulled out his phone and called for his cousin Frankie to come get him.

"We'll take you home," Misha said, patting me on the back like I was some terrified little kid who'd wandered too far from her mommy and had gotten lost. I suppose I did freak out a little bit about the cops busting the party.

"I don't live that far from this neighborhood. I can walk," I said.

"Are you sure?" he said.

"Yeah, but thanks for helping me escape."

He kissed me and said he'd talk to me later.

***

The spring band concert was held on a Tuesday evening in the Fairfield gymnasium. Even though I'd brought the paper home about the concert before spring break, Dad didn't bring it up until the night before.

"Do you want us to come to your band program?" he asked after dinner on Monday.

Of course, I wanted him to come. I wanted him to be a part of the first thing I'd done well since Mom died. But I wasn't going to beg.

"It's up to you if you want to come," I said. Then I instantly regretted it. I was afraid if he really thought he had a choice he'd decide to stay home and drink all night instead of listening to a bunch of teenagers attempt to make music.

"I really want to come," he said, patting me on the back.

Dad went all out for my band concert. Both he and Joey wore dress pants and pressed shirts. And Dad was sober. I could tell how nervous he was driving to the school. He kept reaching over and fidgeting with Joey, trying to keep his hair from sticking out every which way. All of this was probably the nicest thing Dad had done for me in a long time.

Considering how nervous most of us were, the concert actually went pretty well. Two people had solos; Kimberly Stark on the flute and Misha on the saxophone. Kimberly was pretty good, but Misha was a dream on the saxophone. He meshed so well into the instrument that it was hard to tell where Misha ended and the saxophone began. Music flowed through every pore of his body. He knew how to muffle the notes so that even when he played classical music it still sounded like a smoky blues song.

After the concert Dad took us to Dairy Queen and each of us got a banana split. Anyone walking in off the street would have looked at us and believed we were just like any other family stopping for ice cream. I almost choked on my banana as I thought of that. That was probably why I always suspected the worst now when I looked at people I didn't know. I looked at strangers driving in traffic and eating at restaurants and wondered what horrible secrets lay just beyond their front doors. How many of them were beating their kids, stealing from their boss, or slowly drinking themselves to death?

***

It was only May but an early heat wave had covered Indiana like a scratchy wool blanket. Everyone at Fairfield was just trying to hang on until the first week of June. Between third and fourth period I heard a girl in the hall yell out, "I can't wait until summer break! I'm tired of lookin' at y'all!"

Someone yelled back, "Same to you!"

I headed to the girls' restroom near the gym. Vivica and I had gotten into the habit of reapplying our make-up after third period in this particular restroom. Dozens of girls with hormones jumping like corn kernels in hot oil were all crammed into a restroom that smelled like it hadn't been cleaned in a week. A combination like that was bound to unleash trouble, but throw Dani into the mix and it was a recipe for disaster.

"Liza, let me borrow your mascara," Vivica said, holding out her hand for my bottle of black extra lush.

"Who are you all of a sudden?" Dani's voice boomed in the tiny bathroom. "Little Betsy thinks she's tough Liza now, even though she can't even fight her own battles."

I didn't care what people thought anymore so I blurted out the first thing that came to my mind. "Shut the crap up!" didn't have a lot of power behind it, but it was the only thing I could think of at the moment.

Dani, however, let me have it with a string of profanities that seemed to go on for almost a minute. And then the prewar dance began. We side-stepped each other a few times and got our footing while the other girls split into two sides. Then our eyes locked. That was when I remembered Mary Frances and lurched into animal instinct. I attacked Dani like an alley cat on a moonless night.

Being in the midst of a fight wasn't as awful as I'd thought it would be. In fact, I couldn't feel anything. The only thing painful about it was the screaming in the restroom, so loud it hurt my eardrums. I knew, however, that after the fight was over, I'd be in pain.

When it became apparent Dani wasn't going to have an easy win, one of her friends stepped in and broke us up.

"Teachers are going to call the cops," she said.

Dani backed up and nodded, bleeding from her eyebrow. "We'll have to find another time and place to finish this," she said.

I was surprised her friends hadn't just helped Dani take me down. Then I got a good look around the restroom. I saw that a lot more girls were standing along with Vivica on my side. Dani and her girls must have known that if this turned into a full-fledged brawl they wouldn't have won.

Then the bell rang and everyone hurried out into the hall, except for me. There had been at least twenty girls in the restroom and every one of them would get a tardy in fourth period. I was left standing alone, staring into the mirror. Even more shocking than the fact that I had held my own against Dani was the face staring back at me.

So much had changed in just a few months. My eyes looked darker and there were tiny lines around my mouth that hadn't been there before. The most surprising was the expression I had. A permanent scowl seemed to be etched into my face.

Chapter Sixteen

The next day Grandma came over with a plastic tub full of food. Joey had called her and told her that he was sick of eating popcorn and pretzel sticks for dinner. He requested a large chocolate cake. He figured since the cake was something homemade, she'd bring one over. He didn't know our grandma very well.

She brought over baked chicken, steamed vegetables, and fruit, and then sat there and made him eat some. He said he was full after one strawberry and a few grapes. Then he stomped off to his bedroom.

I went to bed a few hours after Grandma left. I tried not to think of her and the way she looked as she paraded around the house with her sunken cheeks, the wrinkled lips, and the anger at Dad that was spilling over to the rest of us. Sure, she'd gotten rid of Abbie, but she only did it for Mom's sake. I could still see the bitterness in her eyes so sharp they were like shrouds of broken glass.

I fell asleep with those eyes burning in my mind. That night I dreamed more than I remembered dreaming in years. I saw the kids in fourth period English and all the pizza I'd eaten during the last six months set out along an endless table.

After that I floated deep into the past; Queen of Angels, my kindergarten teacher, and Joey as a baby. The last thing I remembered dreaming about was Grandma, this time at Mom's funeral. I watched from my front row seat as she leaned over the casket and cried, "My baby! My baby!" She acted like Mom had been a little girl in pigtails who'd let go of her hand and ran out into traffic.

I shot up in bed. I knew I'd been dreaming but I suddenly knew that what I'd been dreaming about had actually happened. I couldn't understand why I would remember it now, and had blocked it out for all these months. And how come I had remembered it in a dream? I tried to convince myself it was just a dream that seemed real.

"No, it did happen," I whispered. "Grandma did fall on the casket and wail for her baby."

It was strange that I would suddenly remember that now. What else had my brain silently tucked away? I feared that this was just a crack in the dam, that all the memories immediately following Mom's death would soon come flooding back. Perhaps this would be the Red Sea that I would ultimately drown in.

I couldn't take it anymore. I needed a diversion, some sort of temporary escape from what my life had become. A few nights later I made sure Joey was stuffed full of anything and everything he would eat so he'd sleep through the night.

I thought about calling Vivica and seeing if her sister would take us somewhere. But then I looked at the clock and saw that it was almost ten, and being a school night, I decided to just go to bed.

By the time I changed clothes and brushed my teeth I noticed that someone had texted me. It was Misha. "Want 2 go for a ride" the message said. I could hear his bluesy voice in my head as I read the words.

I texted back and quickly got dressed again. Dad was in his bedroom with his door closed and Joey had been in bed for an hour now. They were both in an artificially induced sleep, one with alcohol, the other with carbohydrates. I could have blared music and danced around the living room and neither one of them would have woken up.

"My cuz Frankie is driving will pick u up in 15," the next text said.

Ten minutes later I walked through the living room, slowly opened and shut the front door and waited on the porch. I patted the key in my pocket, making sure it was still there before twisting the knob and locking the door.

There was a crescent moon out, with enough light that I could see my reflection in the glass of the front door. After I fluffed my hair and quickly reapplied another layer of hot pink lip gloss, I heard the dull roar of an engine coming down the street.

They pulled into the end of the drive, but didn't come all the way up. It was as if they knew how to do this. They probably had plenty of experience sneaking girls out of the house late at night.

Misha got out of the front and climbed in the back with me. "How you doing?" he said as we situated ourselves in the back.

"I'm good," I said. I didn't want to whine in front of Frankie and Misha.

Frankie drove slow, until we got to the next street. Then he took off like it was the start of the Indy 500. The music went from barely audible to a level where I could feel the sound pounding inside my body.

I felt free and giddy in the backseat of Frankie's Grand Am, the wind rushing through the open window and tangling my hair. For the first time in months, I think I was actually happy there with the wind against my face and Misha's arm draped over my shoulder. Thirty seconds was about as long as my happiness lasted. Then time shifted, along with Misha's arm, and along came his fingers like a crab crawling inside of my shirt. I shivered and he must have felt it.

"Are you okay?" he asked.

"Sure," I said. But I really didn't mean it. The look on my face must have said what I couldn't -- that I was confused about a guy's fingers inching along my shirt and that I didn't have a mom to guide me through the minefield of adolescence and hormonally charged boys.

He leaned over and kissed me, his lips brushing against the corner of my mouth. Then he stopped, and made no attempt to do anything beyond the kiss. I was relieved, but unsure of what it all meant. Was Misha genuinely a nice guy? Or did he have another girlfriend who had no problem going beyond kissing even if they barely knew each other?

During the next hour an array of colorful characters were in and out of the front seat. Frankie had to pick up a friend from work and drop him off somewhere else. Then there were the mysterious errands where he had to drop off things and pick something else up.

Between the errands we stopped at McDonalds and Misha and I scrounged up enough change from our pockets to split a large order of fries.

After Frankie got a phone call and said he had to go to the other side of town, he suggested it was time to take me home. It was just as well. I was tired and had to get up for school the next morning. Of course, so did Misha, but I didn't think getting a good night's sleep was on his list of priorities. In fact, I had no trouble at all imagining them driving around all night, stopping for a quick change of clothes, and then pulling up in front of Fairfield five minutes before the first bell.

Chapter Seventeen

I saw her in the hall, leaning casually against the lockers as if nothing had happened. Tara was back and drawing a crowd of boys around her between second and third period. She looked paler, thinner, and when she leaned over to get a book out of her locker, I could see bruises larger than silver dollars on her lower back.

I'd heard that she'd spent the last thirty days in the Allen County Juvenile Center, otherwise known as ACJC. Supposedly, kids tougher than Dani could barely survive that place. I could only imagine what would happen to someone like Tara, a girl who was too beautiful for a place like that, and the other girls who would hate her for it. Tara was mentally tough. She could think circles around most kids and had a poison tongue to match. But I wasn't sure if those skills would be of much use at ACJC.

As I walked by her locker, I quickly looked away but she'd already seen me.

"So, what are you guys doing in that lame gym class?" she said.

I wanted to keep on walking, but I couldn't pretend I didn't see her now.

"We've been playing badminton," I said. "It isn't too bad."

A kid with a fake tattoo on his cheek walked by and tapped Tara on the shoulder. "I heard you took some vacation time at ACJC," he said with a smirk.

"Yeah, you should have been there," she shot back. "It was a thrill a minute. We got room service, a Jacuzzi, the works."

He chuckled and kept walking. At least she hadn't lost her sense of humor.

"So, what's been happening at this dump?" she said. "Tell me what fights I missed, the hook-ups, the break-ups, give me the scoop."

I was surprised that I was her lifeline at Fairfield and that she didn't have any other connections. I told her everything that was going on and we actually got caught up in the conversation. Since she was keeping me from being on time to my next class, I asked her what I really wanted to know.

"What did you do to get arrested?" I said.

She looked right at me and said, "I robbed some of the houses in the neighborhood." She was casual when she said it, like she'd borrowed a loaf of bread from someone and had forgotten to tell them about it.

"And I threatened a little kid who woke up and caught me. I told him I'd come back in the middle of the night and stab him if he told anyone."

I took a deep breath to steady myself. I didn't want her to think what she said shocked me. Then she started listing off the names of people in our neighborhood she'd stolen things from. She said she took antique jewelry from the Benson's and tools from Steve Turley and then sold the stuff to gang members she met under the Maumee Bridge.

But I couldn't stop thinking about her threatening a little kid. I didn't think she'd ever actually stab a kid, and if she had she wouldn't have been sent back to Fairfield. But I had no doubt that she'd threaten to do it. I could see her taking perverse pleasure in scaring a little kid out of his mind.

"How did they catch you?" I asked, dying to know if the kid had actually told on her.

"Old lady Krill had a security camera in her house," she said, rolling her eyes. "Who would think in an average neighborhood like ours that anyone would have a camera?"

"Girls, you need to get to class," one of the assistant principals said as he walked briskly past us. I looked around and noticed there wasn't anyone left in the hall. I didn't even realize the bell had rang. Tara turned and went one way and I went the other.

I imagined Tara, the lady cat burglar, in a pair of black, skin tight pants and a black turtleneck slipping in and out of houses as light as a whisper. I could see her moving up from the gangs of the Maumee

River to high-end jewel thieves in Europe. She'd hit the mansions late at night, slinking under an array of high-tech lasers like a Chinese acrobat to steal diamonds and rubies. Then again, if she couldn't slip past old Mrs. Krill and her security camera what chance did she have in the big time?

I didn't see much of Tara after that. She missed a lot of school during the next few weeks. Supposedly she was gone for counseling sessions and court dates. Then one day she was gone for good. The gym teacher said she'd been withdrawn from the school. It was then that I wondered if she really did stab that kid.

***

Dorothy Atkins and her husband, Frank, had spent every Saturday in May working in their yard. It didn't look like June was going to be any different. While Dorothy planted flowers along the front porch, Frank meticulously filled the fertilizer machine. As I stood in our garage I watched as he wiped the handle and then made sure the front tire was straight. Then I realized something wasn't right. Anytime they'd been outside doing work Tara had always been with them. "Forced labor," she called it. In the fall they made her rake leaves and in the winter she shoveled snow.

Then I saw the new boy. He ran out of the garage and into the yard with a rake. Dorothy pointed a finger at the flower bed across from the garage and immediately the boy ran over and began combing the fresh dirt back and forth with the rake. His shiny blonde hair shimmered in the bright sun while he quickly smoothed the dirt. He was working so hard. I could see his arms quivering from across the street. New foster kids always tried too hard to please. It was obvious he was desperate to make it in his new placement. Tara had given up on making it anywhere.

When I saw that Dorothy was heading toward the edge of the lawn I went down and looked in the mailbox, even though I'd already gotten the mail an hour earlier. I turned around when I knew she was close enough that she'd wave. I walked toward her as she tossed pebbles from the yard back into the driveway.

Dorothy looked at me like it had been four years instead of four months since she'd last seen me close up. I'd lost weight. My hair was three different colors and none of them matched. I had four earrings and a fake tattoo on my neck.

"What happened to Tara?" I said, smiling at the new boy.

Dorothy shook her head. "It was a good thing we got rid of that girl when we did. She was bad news."

"Why? What did she do?" I asked. I pretended Tara hadn't told me about burglarizing the neighborhood and threatening some kid.

"That girl stole, lied about it, and even threatened the Jenkins boy. After all that we still gave that girl another chance, and what did she do? She got drunk at our family reunion and made a spectacle of herself. It was the last straw."

Stealing and threatening little kids they could handle, but

embarrassing Dorothy at a family get-together was apparently too much to take. "Where is Tara now?" I asked, waiting for some elaborate story.

Dorothy rolled her eyes and flipped up her palms. "Who knows?"

I could only imagine where Tara was now. Maybe she'd ran away and joined the gang of bandits living under the Maumee Bridge. If anyone could survive like that it was Tara. I could see her flying through downtown Fort Wayne on the back of a motorcycle, weaving around the fountains at the open-air mall, and snatching rich ladies' purses.

After her gang had eaten a good meal off the spoils they'd ride out to the south side of town and distribute the rest of the money to the poor and homeless before returning to their kingdom under the bridge.

"So, she ran away?" I said.

"Oh, no," Dorothy said with a bitter laugh. "Children's Services took her away."

That put an end to my romantic vision of what had happened to Tara. She most likely had been placed in another foster home.

"Buddy here has been a dream," Dorothy said, pointing to her blonde, blue-eyed darling still pounding the dirt with the rake.

Before Mom died, I never would have paid attention to people like Buddy or Tara. It wasn't that I thought I was better than they were, I just wouldn't have thought of them at all. But now that my own ship had sunk, it was easier to see all the wreckage around me. People who sailed through life on top of the waves seldom noticed the carnage that lay beneath the surface.

"He's the sweetest little boy," she said with a big smile. "That girl was just a constant problem."

I thought it was interesting how she was "that" girl now instead of Tara. I don't think Dorothy had called her by her first name once since we'd been talking. Dorothy was in such a good mood about getting rid of Tara and bringing home Buddy that she gave me a big basket full of homemade baked bread, biscuits, and chocolate chip cookies. We were so stuffed from all the starch and carbohydrates that Joey and I went to bed early.

That night I dreamed I was flying when a buzzing sound came rushing into my ears. Being able to fly was a common dream, but one that I rarely had anymore. It seemed that my wings had been temporarily clipped and I'd been grounded for months.

Now that I was dreaming it again, I wanted to hang onto it for as long as possible. But the ringing in my ears had become too loud to stay asleep. I was flying over the city of Fort Wayne, barely clearing the Summit building but easily passing over the Lincoln Tower.

When I completely woke up, the phone was still ringing.

I glanced at my clock. It was a few minutes past two. Where was Dad? Why wasn't he answering the phone? I stumbled out of bed, tripping on a pile of dirty laundry on my way to the door. I stopped and steadied myself while hanging onto the door knob. The fact that the phone was still ringing wasn't a good sign. Had someone else died? A prank caller wouldn't have let it ring this long. After finally making it to the kitchen I almost dropped the phone while trying to pick it up.

"Hello," I said in a dreary voice.

"Is this Betsy?" the caller asked.

Actually, I was Liza. What was so hard about that? But I was too tired to argue.

"Yeah, who is this?"

"It's your Uncle Evan."

Suddenly I was wide awake, running to Dad's bedroom with the phone still clutched in my hand. Just as I feared, his bed was empty. He'd never come home.

"Has Dad been in a wreck! Is he dead!" I screamed. When I looked up Joey was standing next to me, rubbing his eyes.

"Listen, your dad's not dead and he hasn't been in a wreck," Evan said.

I sighed, but didn't say anything. I thought maybe this had something to do with Abbie. I could see her in an angry rage shooting him, or getting someone to beat him up.

"Your dad's not hurt," Evan assured me. "But he's been arrested for drunk driving."

I almost dropped the phone. For some strange reason it was the last thing I expected to hear. A wave of weariness swept over my body, trying to pull me down.

"Where is he?" I said.

"Here in Fort Wayne. He's at the downtown lockup."

There was an awkward silence and I thought, what does he expect me to do about it? Did he think I was going to drive down there and bail him out?

"I just wanted to make sure you knew what was going on so you wouldn't be worried or wonder where he was."

I felt like telling him that I hadn't been the least bit worried, that I'd been peacefully flying over Fort Wayne when I'd been so rudely interrupted. And if I had the chance, I'd go back. I'd fly right over the police station without looking down once.

"I'll bail him out as soon as I can and bring him home," Evan said.

"Thanks," I mumbled. Joey was tugging on my shirt, asking what was going on.

"Do you need anything?" Evan asked.

I almost laughed out loud. He was asking this after all these months, and at two in the morning while Dad was in jail? I should have said, yeah, I need a new life, someone who gives a crap, and why don't you pick up a bag of chips when you bring it all over. But I said, "No, we're good. Thanks for calling and letting us know what's happened."

After I hung up the phone, I thought about telling Joey some lame story about Dad having car trouble. But I figured he'd find out anyway, so I told him the truth. He rubbed his eyes again and went back to bed.

The next morning when I got up, Dad was home and making coffee. I hadn't even heard him come in. I figured he would be freaking out over the drunk driving arrest but he wasn't. He was puttering around the kitchen like nothing had even happened.

Chapter Eighteen

I loved July. It was miles away from both the end and the beginning of school. Nothing too difficult ever seemed to happen in July. I glanced at the Atkins' house as I strolled down the drive to get the mail. The garage door was shut, which meant they were gone. Now that they had Buddy, they were gone all the time. They were always taking him to the zoo, the park, and family get-togethers. I figured they would probably end up adopting him. It was all too good to be true. How long did they think it could last?

But as I pulled the mail out of the box, I quickly realized that my ominous premonition hadn't been about the Atkins. I held the envelope in my hands, thinking that even after everything we had already lost, we were in store for more. The foreclosure notice was written across the front in big print. First and Fifth Loan Company was printed in small neat letters across the top of the envelope.

Usually the bill from the mortgage company came in a plain white envelope, as inconspicuous as a blade of grass. This month it came in a bright yellow envelope. I went inside and dropped the mail on the kitchen table next to Dad, making sure the yellow envelope was on top.

"Is everything okay?" I said.

"Sure. Why wouldn't it be?" he said, digging into a bowl of cornflakes.

Nothing seemed to faze him anymore. Drunk driving arrests, getting urgent notices from the mortgage company -- nothing was a big deal. He put his hand over it and pushed it under a stack of papers on the table.

That night I pulled a bottle of sleeping pills out of the kitchen cabinet and stared at them. What could be the harm in taking a few? For a second I contemplated taking them all at once. I could slip off to sleep and find my mother somewhere on the other side. But every ounce of my Catholic upbringing screamed back that I wouldn't find peace and tranquility waiting on the other side of a suicide.

That's when it hit me. That's when I knew beyond a shadow of a doubt that my mother would never commit suicide. But I had to get proof. If the police wouldn't talk to me, I figured the emergency workers who had been at the crash site when Mom died could possibly give me some answers. But as far as contacting the EMS or any medical personnel who had worked with Mom, that would have to wait. There was another emergency that was about to strike our family.

Only a few days after the foreclosure notice arrived, what I feared had finally happened. Joey and I were at the kitchen table eating peanut butter and jelly sandwiches when Dad pulled out a chair and sat down between us. I could tell he was nervous. He was rubbing his hands together and looking everywhere except at our faces.

"I have something important to talk to you guys about."

The last time Dad said something like this I had to change schools.

"What is it?" Joey asked. He took another big bite of his sandwich. At his age he didn't understand the potential tragedy in the words, "I have something to talk to you about."

"We're going to have to move," Dad said.

"Where are we going?" Joey said with his mouth full.

He still didn't get it. He seemed to think we were moving up, heading toward a real nice neighborhood or something.

Then Dad said something about bank statements that didn't make sense and how bureaucracies could really mess up your life. The whole time Joey kept chewing and I still hadn't said a word. Dad kept hedging his words, talking in circles and trying to make it sound like anything other than what it was. I couldn't stand it anymore and just came out and said what I knew had happened.

"You mean you stopped paying the mortgage," I said, sounding more like a spouse than a daughter.

"Absolutely not," he insisted. "I have direct deposit and somehow the money got transferred to the wrong account."

Later we would find out that even though the bank had been

taking money directly from Dad's paychecks, he had initially filled out the wrong paper work. They would insist that they'd been sending notices telling him the mortgage wasn't being paid and that he hadn't responded. On top of that, Dad had a bank credit card he'd stopped making payments on, and even if they found out where the mortgage money had gone funds were needed to cover the credit card. It was basically a mess that would take longer than expected to figure out.

"It will take us a few weeks to sort everything out," the lady at the bank told Dad over the phone. What she didn't seem to understand was that the people holding our mortgage were already in the process of foreclosing on our house. We didn't have the luxury of a few weeks to sort everything out.

That evening Dad stood at my bedroom door and told me to start getting things packed.

"When are we leaving?" I said, trying not to cry. I looked around at all the things in my bedroom, and then out in the living room. How long would it take me to pack what had taken our family years to accumulate? A week? Several weeks?

"Tomorrow morning," he said without emotion. "We have to be out by nine."

We *have* to be out by nine? What was going to happen if we weren't? Where the police going to drag us out kicking and screaming? Dad didn't stick around long enough for me to ask. He went to his bedroom with a bottle and shut the door.

There was no way I could get everything packed by tomorrow

morning. And what about Mom's things that we wanted to keep? There were Victorian dolls Joey and I had gotten her for Christmas last year and her Hummel figurine collection. And she had hand-made jewelry and dozens of tiny crafts she'd collected over the years. It would take us days working nonstop to properly wrap and pack everything.

But there was no use trying to explain all that to Dad now. It was already way past time to go to bed and Dad was already way past drunk. As soon as Dad had gone to bed, I tried to pack a little bit of everything, but I knew it was like trying to take one piece from a dozen different puzzles and hoping it would somehow all fit together.

Before going to bed I stuffed my purse with the essentials; social security cards and birth certificates for Joey and me, a few pictures of Mom, and about thirty dollars in cash.

Then I looked on my desk and saw my Bible, the one I'd gotten for my first Communion, laying silent and untouched for so long. I quickly stuffed it into a bag with some jewelry, a Hummel, and a few other fragments of a life gone by, hoping it was all more pieces that would someday fit together to make a normal life.

Normal -- I hadn't heard or thought of that word in ages. Before turning out the light I looked up the word normal on my phone and read what Webster had to say.

Normal: 1). Conforming with an accepted standard or norm; natural; usual.

At eight the next morning Dad stood out in the living room and called for Joey and me. "Are you guys ready?" His voice was gruff.

"Yeah," I said.

Joey didn't respond so Dad stepped into his bedroom and told him we were leaving.

"I'm not going!" Joey cried.

Dad tried to be nice, tried to make a little kid understand as best he could. It wasn't working out very well. He tried to make everything sound intellectual and distant.

"The mortgage fund was mismanaged at the corporate level," he said.

Then he mumbled something that didn't make any sense at all. Lies were always complicated. The truth was usually simple, bare and to the point, and therefore so often avoided.

He should have just said, I was out of my mind with grief, drunk half the time and not paying attention to what I was doing. But he couldn't bring himself to say it. I don't think he believed any of it himself.

In less than ten minutes we filled the trunk and climbed into the car. Dad started the engine and I saw that there was less than half a tank of gas. We only had a few boxes and suitcases packed and Dad was living on a credit card that was probably going to get canceled any day now.

Joey started crying again when Dad put the car in reverse. This time Dad wasn't so understanding. "Shut up! Just shut up!" he bellowed. Dad had never told Joey or me to shut up. It surprised Joey so much that he actually stopped crying.

Dad's shoulders slumped down and his hands slid to the bottom of the steering wheel. He must have felt guilty, but not enough to actually say he was sorry.

"Listen," he said, leaning over the car seat. "Everything is going to be okay. We're going to stay at a motel for a few days, a week at the most, just until I can get everything straightened out at the bank."

Joey didn't say anything after that. He just sat in the back seat with a scowl on his face. Then Dad started telling Joey that staying at the motel would be like going on vacation. As we drove out of the neighborhood, past a cluster of large maples, their leaves lush and full in the height of summer, I almost started believing it myself. Staying at a motel for a few days would be like a vacation, maybe there would even be a pool.

But the Breeze-By Inn off Highway Five was a dingy little motel with no other buildings or houses close by. The nearest convenience store was about half a mile down the road. It looked like the Bates Motel from the movie Psycho, a place where serial killers found easy victims. It definitely wasn't like being on vacation. Breeze-By Inn was a dirty motel full of vagrants, addicts, and homeless people -- people like us.

While Dad was checking us in I stood outside the office and called Grandma Haynes.

I told her what had happened and begged her to take Mom's

figurines, the computer in the den, and the rest of the clothes we couldn't pack and put it all in storage so it wouldn't be taken away when they came to foreclose on the house.

She didn't question what I was saying or even ask to talk to Dad. I wondered if she already knew what had happened. She'd probably seen this coming for months.

"I'll take care of things," she said stiffly. "Are you and Joey okay?"

I looked around at the abandoned cars, the broken shutters, the broken people who were scattered along the front steps and picnic tables like dust. "Yeah, I guess," I said.

I turned off the phone just as Dad came out.

"This way," he said, shuffling a plastic card between his fingers.

We were in the upper level, room twenty-seven. The door was rusty and warped and it took a few minutes for Dad to get the card to work. I don't remember many details after that. The constant din of the TV, eating stale chips and playing meaningless card games with Joey took up several hours. The entire first day passed in a blur.

"I guess it's time for bed," Dad said when it started getting dark out.

There were two double beds, and thankfully Joey slept with Dad. It was still weird sleeping in the same room with my Dad and my brother. Dad snored something awful and Joey tossed and turned and moaned all night.

I'd brought the sleeping pills and considered taking one. But I had to stay alert in a place like this. There were people playing heavy metal music next door. I could hear an argument coming from the parking lot. I had to be able to wake up quickly and think clearly if necessary.

Chapter Nineteen

The next morning, I woke up to find Dad pacing around the room while talking on the phone. As soon as he saw that I was awake he turned and faced the window. He said something I couldn't understand and then turned back around.

"I've got to go to court this morning. Uncle Evan is going to take me."

By the time I got dressed, brushed my teeth and came out of the bathroom, Uncle Evan was standing in our motel room. He'd brought us doughnuts and a quart of milk. He set everything on the dresser and told us to help ourselves.

"I want all the jelly-filled," Joey said, grabbing the box.

Thankfully, Evan brought six doughnuts, two of each kind. He'd raised two kids of his own and knew everything had to be split evenly down the middle or it would be war.

While Joey and I were devouring our doughnuts, Evan stepped

outside the motel room and smoked a cigarette. Dad went out to join him, telling us he'd be back in before they left. When I heard them starting to argue I turned down the TV and stood by the window.

"I can't hear!" Joey whined.

"Here, eat the rest of my jelly doughnut," I said, practically stuffing it in his mouth.

It shut him up long enough for me to hear most of what they were saying.

"Since you got arrested, you're not even supposed to be driving," Evan said. "What if you would have gotten pulled over with the kids?"

"I'm a single dad and it's not like I've got family helping me out," Dad said.

"What do you think I'm doing right now?" Evan yelled back.

"I could have hired a taxi for a ride into town," Dad said smugly.

He wasn't even admitting everything to Evan. The cost of a taxi from here to the courthouse probably would have maxed out what was left on his credit card.

"I'm doing everything I can," Evan said, his voice softer this time. "At least everything you'll let me do."

I barely got away from the window before Dad came storming back inside.

"I'll be gone for most of the morning. Keep the door locked," he said before leaving.

Joey had packed some markers and paper and I spent the next few hours drawing while he watched TV and read a comic book. It was almost one when they came back to the motel. I could hear them in the parking lot arguing as soon as they got out of the car.

"You always blamed me for everything that went wrong at home!" Evan yelled.

"You were always the one who was out getting drunk and doing drugs. When I got to high school, they figured I'd end up the same way. They barely let me out of the house thanks to you!" Dad retaliated.

"Yeah, and you didn't do anything to help me. You told on me, turned me in, and ignored me as if I didn't exist. And now the tables are turned and you don't understand why I don't give up everything to help you?"

"So that's what this is, payback?" Dad said.

"You don't know what it's like to have your only brother turn on you and abandon you. And then you had the audacity to marry the perfect girl and have the perfect family."

"Are you out of your mind? I wasn't even thirteen yet when everything happened to you."

Then, they got quiet, barely talking above a whisper and I couldn't make out what they were saying. But I understood the basic premise of it all now. Evan was the original family screw-up, the one Dad had ignored back when his own life had been wonderful. Now Dad was the one who was sinking and his brother had attempted to help, had at least made the effort. But there was so much bitterness and baggage between them now and it was pretty much useless.

A few minutes later Dad came back in and pulled out his wallet, fingered through a few ones and fives, and then said, "I'll be back in about ten minutes."

"Where are you going now?" I demanded. I couldn't take it anymore. What was he going to do to me anyway? Send me to my room? Not let me go out and have any fun with my friends?

"I'll be back in ten minutes," he said again stiffly. He slammed the door and left.

He was almost certainly going to buy alcohol. I almost called the cops and turned him in. But I was afraid where Joey and I would end up next. The thought of dropping much lower on the food chain terrified me.

When he came back, Dad at least had the decency to sit out in the parking lot and get drunk in the car. He came back in when the bottle was empty and went to bed. It wasn't even dark yet and I was the only one still awake.

While Joey slept and Dad was passed out, I stepped outside the room with my cell phone. I knew Dad had stopped paying all the bills so I wasn't sure how much longer it would be working. I texted Misha and told him I was going to call. Thankfully, everything was still working.

"I haven't seen you since right after school ended," Misha said. "I thought maybe we could get together, hang out at the mall or something."

"That sounds great," I said. "But we're out of town on vacation right now." I hated lying but I just couldn't tell him where I was.

"Must be nice to be rich," he said with a laugh.

"Whatever," I said, trying to sound casual. "So, what have you been up to?"

"Been hanging out with Frankie and last week I jammed with Harris."

Matt Harris was a high school kid who played the drums. With Misha on the sax, the two of them together sounded like professional musicians.

"Sounds like fun," I said.

We talked for a few more minutes about the last movie he went to see and the bands playing at the Summer Jam Festival.

"Call me when you get back in town," he said.

"Sure. Talk to you later."

I turned off the phone. Yeah, Misha, I'll call you when I get back in town, back to some galaxy I recognize and out of this black hole I've been sucked into.

I would find out later that Dad pleaded guilty to misdemeanor drunk driving, lost his license for six months, was ordered to perform forty hours of community service, and had to attend a weekend class about the dangers of excessive drinking. Thankfully, the judge gave him a hardship license since he was a single parent. He could drive to work, to the grocery once a week, stuff like that. But getting to work or the grocery wasn't his biggest problem anymore.

Chapter Twenty

The next morning at seven the motel manager was banging on our door. I was having a bizarre dream about falling into a dirty river. I was better off waking up. But when I rolled over and got a good look at Dad, I wished I could have kept on floating down that muddy river. When he sat up in bed I was shocked by his appearance. His skin was pasty gray and his eyes looked like they had each grown a size smaller.

The guy kept beating on the door, calling out for Eric Kimmel.

"Your credit card has been canceled," the man yelled from the other side of the door. "You have to be out by ten unless you have cash."

I knew Dad didn't have enough cash on him to pay for food, gas and another night at the motel.

He finally stumbled out of bed and ran after the guy. "Here, I've got another credit card."

I got out of bed and pressed my face against the window, watching as Dad ran after the guy. This was beyond pathetic. The front door of our room was still hanging open.

The guy kept walking and shaking his head. "Your credit is no good. Cash only."

Dad came back into the room and slammed the door behind him.

"Out by ten or I'm calling the cops," the guy yelled back.

Since his fight with Uncle Evan, there wasn't anyone left in Fort Wayne he wasn't too proud to stay with. That left one option -- tent city. At least Dad didn't tell Joey to look at it like we were going on a camping trip.

He left Joey and me at McDonalds with enough money to split an order of hotcakes and sausage while he did some "shopping". He came back an hour later with a small tent and three sleeping bags stuffed in the back of the car. I didn't see shopping bags or a receipt for anything.

"Where are we going?" I said.

"Get in the car," was his only response.

Dad turned the radio on low and started driving. He was making a lot of turns, driving deeper into the downtown area. We finally got far enough away from anything I recognized. I could hardly believe this was still part of Fort Wayne. The streets were littered with garbage and rows of abandoned warehouses with broken windows formed the backdrop. There were parts of town that no one ever went to for a reason. We crossed a bridge over a creek, and there it was -- Fort Wayne's own tent city.

"This is worse than a homeless shelter," I grumbled. "I'd rather sleep in the car."

"There's not enough room for all of us in the car," Dad said. "Besides, it's only for a few nights. Once I get back to work and get my next paycheck, we'll go somewhere else."

Dad had taken a temporary leave of absence from his job so I wasn't sure when he was going to get paid or how long the money would last. But that wasn't my biggest concern at the moment.

So, this was what my life had come to? Sleazy motels and sleeping in a parking lot? In some ways it was a relief. We'd hit rock bottom and there wasn't anything left to be afraid of. That's what I thought until I finally got a good look at this place.

The tents were side by side, set up right next to one another in the parking lot. There were spaces no wider than an average hallway between the rows of tents. Next to the parking lot was an open field of unmowed grass. That was the bathroom.

Most of the tents were threadbare and flimsy, just like the people who lived in them. There were small fires burning all over the place and lines of clothes hung up and drying. I had no idea where anyone would wash clothes in a place like this.

"Come on, kids, help me with the tent," Dad said, as he started pulling things out of the trunk.

It didn't take long for the three of us to find a spot, put up the tent, and unpack our things. No one even paid attention to us while we were getting ourselves situated. No one came over and held out a hand and said, "Hi, I'm Joe Smith. I live next door. Let me know if I can help with anything."

For dinner we ate cereal from the box and washed it down with warm soda. All the sugar gave me a headache.

"We might as well go to bed," Dad said with a sigh. He opened the flap on the tent and looked out across the parking lot.

"How am I going to brush my teeth," Joey said in a whiny voice.

It was a shame that he finally cared about personal hygiene when he couldn't do anything about it.

"I'll get some bottled water tomorrow so you can brush your teeth," Dad said.

I laid my head on the small, lumpy pillow and squeezed my eyes shut. I wanted to fall asleep as quickly as possible and pass the night away in a blur of dreams. For a few sweet moments I had almost drifted off, then the screaming started. It sounded like it was coming from the west end of the parking lot. The loud voices and the swearing didn't scare me as much as it might have a year ago. Then we heard gunshots. There was more screaming, and then Joey started crying. It was more of a slow sob than a stream of tears. After that we heard a police siren in the distance.

I scooted my sleeping bag next to Joey's and tried to comfort him the best I could.

He finally fell asleep with his face buried in my arm. The top of my arm was gooey from his tears and runny nose, but I didn't dare move because I was afraid he'd wake up and start crying again.

The next morning, we found out that the Sisters of Mercy from St. Mary's Church came every few days to pass out cheese sandwiches and bottled water. If they came while we were still here, I was going to ask if I could go with them. I could become a nun, give up my life and serve the poor. At least I wouldn't be living in a stolen tent. But they had just come the day before and wouldn't be here again for at least another day or so.

"I'm thirsty," Joey said.

Dad nodded as he looked out over the parking lot. "I'll go get us some things."

He didn't tell us where he was going or how long he'd be gone, just to keep the inside of the tent zipped and locked. He must have gotten things from other people living in nearby tents because he was back in less than ten minutes.

After looking at what he brought back I knew that was what he had done. The six pack of water he brought back only had four left in it and the package of granola bars was open. While I was eating a cookies and cream granola bar I could hear someone calling our names and the quick click of high heels on the pavement outside the tent. I would have known that firm voice and that quick step anywhere. It was Grandma Haynes.

I opened the tent and stepped outside, Dad and Joey followed behind. I could never remember her being so strong and determined.

Wearing the beautiful lavender suit and silky cream blouse she'd had on at Mom's funeral, Grandma Haynes demanded that Joey and I pack our things and leave with her.

"Are you crazy?" Dad said. "I'm their father and the kids are staying with me."

"You're living in a tent in a parking lot and you're calling me crazy?" Grandma said.

Dad cleared his throat. "It's only temporary. I've got everything under control."

"Yes, I can clearly see how under control everything is," she said, the sarcasm as sharp as the click of her high heels.

I'd told her the house had been foreclosed and I wondered if somehow she'd found out about Dad's DWI. I had no idea how she'd known to come look for us here. It was then that I realized it was Grandma who had called Family and Children's Services when Mr. Frank had come to check on us. Going through the proper channels and calling the authorities wasn't Abbie's style.

But Dad told her to leave, to turn around and go home. She didn't move a muscle. She stood as tall and proud as an old lady could, staring straight at him.

"I've got a court order to take these kids," she said, waving the papers. "And the only way you'll get them back is if you go to rehab and prove you're clean and sober." She'd finally called his bluff. There was nothing else he could do.

Dad nervously looked around to see who was listening. This was so bad that it was embarrassing even in a place like this. Being homeless was one thing, having your kids taken away while everyone watched was the ultimate humiliation.

"You never did want me to marry Kathy," Dad muttered.

"This isn't about you or me anymore. It's about what's best for these kids."

Grandma was on top of her game. She never denied that she didn't want Dad to marry her daughter, and she still managed to come out on top in the war of words.

"Where are we going now?" Joey whimpered.

He couldn't see this for what it was, a chance to start over, a faint light at the end of a long and dreary tunnel. To him, she was just an old lady he barely knew, taking him away from the only parent he had left.

I suppose I'll never forget the way Dad looked when we left him. He was sitting on the ground in front of the tent, his shoulders sagging and his back heaving up and down as he cried into his hands. I kissed him goodbye on the forehead. He wouldn't look up, but he squeezed my hand so tight I thought my fingers would break.

Chapter Twenty-One

The first night we stayed with Grandma she let us do pretty much whatever we wanted. We ate what we wanted, stayed up late, and threw our clothes anywhere. It was almost like living with Dad. But by the second day, everything changed. I suppose she thought one day of transition was enough.

The second evening of our stay at the Hampton Hills Senior Living Community, Grandma summoned us to the kitchen for dinner at six sharp. She set plates that were already full of food in front of Joey and me like we were two-years old. There were perfectly portioned pieces of chicken, broccoli, and a medium-sized baked potato on each of our plates. In a separate bowl for each of us was a small square of red Jello for dessert.

Joey and I just looked at each other.

"I'm not eating this," he said, pushing his plate away.

"Fine, don't eat it," Grandma said calmly. "But you're not going to watch TV or eat anything else the rest of the night unless you eat every bite of your dinner."

Joey started to cry. It was his only line of defense, to pout and make enough racket that Grandma would eventually give in and order pizza, tacos, whatever he wanted just to shut him up. That's what Dad did. He couldn't stand the whining.

Joey cried and begged for almost an hour but Grandma wouldn't budge. She acted like he wasn't even there. I don't know how she put up with it. All of his noise was getting on my nerves so bad that I almost called for pizza delivery a few times. Grandma covered his plate with foil and put it in the fridge. After that he cried himself to sleep on the sofa and I helped her carry him in to bed.

"Do you want to watch anything in particular on TV?" Grandma said when we came back out to the living room.

"No thanks," I said. "I'm getting tired. I think I'll go to bed."

"Good night, Betsy," she said as she kissed me on the cheek.

I didn't even try to bring up that I wanted to be called Liza. There was no way Grandma would ever call me that, and I didn't even care anymore.

The next morning when we got up Grandma had fried eggs, toast, and fruit set on plates for both of us. Joey was so hungry he ate every bite without saying a word.

Grandma had accomplished quite a feat, considering Joey hated eggs and didn't care much for fruit either. It was amazing how quickly she whipped him into shape and got both of us into a regular routine.

But there was barely enough room for three people in her two-bedroom duplex. I wished she still lived in her old house a few miles out of town. She had a big backyard, and a finished basement where we used to watch movies and play pool. But six months after Grandpa died, she sold everything and moved to the duplex.

Grandma was just sixty-three and was one of the younger ones in the place. She would half brag, half complain about her situation, about all the widowed old men who hit on her and asked her out on dates. At least once a day someone at the complex would stop by and visit Grandma. She was part of a garden guild, an exercise group, and a card club. All of her old people friends smelled like medicine and too much soap. I hated it when they came over. And almost all of them, especially the women, would fawn over Joey and me, telling us how cute we were.

One night when Joey and I were in our pajamas, someone started knocking at the door.

"Can you get that?" Grandma called from the bedroom.

I opened the door to find a skinny old man standing there with a silly grin on his face.

"Well, invite him in," Grandma said, walking up behind me.

Bill White looked at least twenty years older than Grandma. He had cheeks that draped like a hound dog and he walked with a cane. Mentally, though, he was still pretty sharp. He was what Grandma called a great conversationalist. He did seem to make her laugh a lot.

But I thought most of what he said was boring and not the least bit funny.

After we'd all been sitting in the living room about fifteen minutes, Bill reached into his pocket and pulled out a handful of candy and offered Joey and me some mints.

"Want some?" he said with a toothless grin.

The candies were individually wrapped but most of them were smashed and had dirt around the edges of the wrapping. It was disgusting.

"No thanks," I said, speaking for both Joey and myself. "We had a big dinner."

"Speaking of dinner," Bill White said, "you still haven't made me your famous fried chicken and mashed potatoes. We could all get together here tomorrow for dinner."

Was this going to be like Abbie all over again? Some deadbeat trying to weasel into our lives, only this time it was the senior citizen version. But unlike Dad, Grandma got rid of this one before it went too far.

"I don't think it's going to work out tomorrow evening, Bill," she said softly. "When I see you at card club next week maybe I'll bring some chicken for you in a cold pack."

He didn't look too happy about it when Grandma told him it was getting late and she was tired. But he was old and frail. What was he going to do about it? Beat her over the head with his cane? He whispered something into her ear. She smiled and then he left.

I'd never been so impressed with an adult as I was with Grandma at that moment. It was obvious that she liked this guy, but she was willing to send him away because she thought it wasn't best for Joey and me if he hung around too much. It was the first time I had felt safe in a long time.

***

The next afternoon it was almost five o'clock when I heard a slow but firm knock at the door. We weren't supposed to answer the door when Grandma was gone, but I figured it was okay since she was just at the next duplex visiting a friend and would be back soon.

I opened the door to find a large, stern-faced policeman staring down at me.

"I'm here to see an Elizabeth Kimmel," the officer said.

"Yeah, that's me," I said. I told him to come inside.

"I'm here to answer some questions regarding your mother's death last October."

My heart began to race, but "Okay," was all I could manage to say. I was surprised that after all this time someone was actually bothering to show up and talk to me.

"It took us a while to find out where you were living," he said pulling papers out of his shirt pocket. "Is there anything in particular you wanted to know?"

I wasn't sure I could even open my mouth and speak. He was a large man and every time he shifted his weight it frightened me.

"I need to know if the crash was really an accident ...or if my mom ran into the truck on purpose. I need to know if she killed herself."

The words sounded so awful that I could barely say them, but he didn't flinch. I suppose as a city police officer he'd seen so much misery and human carnage in his life that he'd hardly bat an eye at the prospect of a depressed woman killing herself in traffic.

"I have copies of the coroner's report and the report filed by the paramedics on the scene of the accident," he said as he unfolded the papers.

He started reading the papers, taking forever to come to any conclusion about what it all meant. Then he looked down at me.

He shook his head, slowly at first, and then more intently. "It wasn't a suicide."

"Are you sure?" I said.

"There are experts whose job it is to examine auto accidents," he said. "They can tell by the skid marks on the road, the angle at which the car and the semi collided, and witness testimony that your mom didn't hit the driver on purpose. She definitely slammed on the breaks."

I'd never felt such relief in all my life. I hadn't realized the weight I'd been carrying until it was suddenly removed. "Who is the witness testimony?" I said.

"The driver in the car that had been behind her. He told police she swerved out of the path of the semi, but he'd crossed the line too far for her to avoid him. Besides that, the report the paramedics filed said she had fought to live." That's when the officer swallowed and looked away, his professionalism momentarily faltering. "They were surprised she hung on as long as she did, considering the extent of her injuries."

"How come it took so long to get all this information to me?" I said.

"Unfortunately, several people die every week in traffic accidents. There are a lot of files and red tape to work through."

"I understand," I said, trying to sound serious and grown-up in front of the officer.

"Is there anything else I can do for you?" he said.

"No," I said. "Thanks for giving me this information."

As soon as he was gone, I stood out on Grandma's front porch, listening as a warm summer wind swept through the trees. I stood there until the wind had carried away all my tears.

Chapter Twenty-Two

I was surprised when Grandma came home from her exercise class and told us we were going to visit Dad. She said we were leaving in twenty minutes.

Joey sighed. "Do we have to dress up?"

"You're fine as you are," Grandma said.

There was a spaghetti stain on the shirt I was wearing. I almost changed it and then decided I didn't need to look nice for Dad. After all, he was the reason we were living in a retirement center and I hadn't seen any of my friends in ages. I didn't need to do him any favors.

On the drive to the rehab facility no one said much. Grandma turned on a jazz station on the radio, the music turned down low. That depressed me even more, making me think of Misha and how much I missed just hanging out with him.

After about fifteen minutes in the car I realized for the first time since she told us where we were going that I was frightened. We were going where alcoholics and drug addicts came to dry out. I imagined that there would be people screaming, beating on the walls, and trying to escape. And Grandma was taking us to a place like this? This was a woman who always said thank-you and please, a woman so refined that she always wore hose with skirts, and never wore white after Labor Day.

"Is Dad okay?" was the only thing I could think to ask.

"He's doing very well," she said, almost smiling.

Later, I found out that the facility was divided into two areas. The first building was where the patients actually went through detox. After the physical withdraw was over they were moved into small, individual apartments where they received counseling.

Visitors under eighteen weren't allowed in the detox center. That was probably why we hadn't seen Dad for over a week. Kids weren't allowed to witness all the shaking and puking.

Forest Parke Rehabilitation Center was about an hour north of Fort Wayne, nestled between a wave of rolling hills and dozens of large, shady trees. It looked like a resort or a camp for spoiled rich kids. I knew places like this were outrageously expensive, some over ten thousand dollars for a thirty day stay. I wondered if Dad's insurance had paid for it or if Grandma had drained her savings account. I didn't want to know.

"Just stay behind me," Grandma instructed when we walked inside.

We waited in a small consultation room that was decorated like the waiting room in a nice doctor's office. About ten minutes later a middle-aged woman opened the door and escorted Dad inside. He was in some sort of uniform, almost like Army clothes. But his hair was like Joey's now, tangled, uncombed, and curly on the ends.

I didn't want to let him hug me. I'd come so far since he'd been gone. I was sleeping regularly, eating good food. Besides, I was still angry with him for lying about Mom and bringing a witch like Abbie into our lives.

He pulled Joey into an embrace with one hand and reached for me with the other. I pulled back and he was too weak to keep hold of me. He pretended not to notice. Grandma sat down first and we all situated ourselves on the matching loveseats.

"Is Grandma taking good care of you?" he said, more of a statement than a question.

I wanted to say, yeah, Dad, it's great living with all the old people. I just love the way they smell and eating Jello with every meal. The only reason I didn't say it was because Grandma was in the room. Even though she hadn't always been my favorite person, if she wouldn't have taken us in, I hated to think where we might have ended up.

"It's fine," I said.

Then he shifted gears and started telling us about things he was doing in rehab, all the meetings and the therapy. But the way he was talking, it was almost like he was making himself out to be some kind of martyr. He told us about all the suffering, how hard it was here and what a survivor he was. I couldn't take it anymore.

"They told us in health class that some alcoholics die when going through detox," I said stiffly. "Has that happened to anyone since you've been here."

He looked at me like I was some sort of sicko who wished misery on other people. But Grandma didn't look shocked at all. She was tired of listening to him, too.

"No, I don't think so," he said softly.

I didn't think his face could get any paler until I said I wanted to talk to him alone.

"Come on, Joey," Grandma said, standing up and pressing out the creases in her skirt. "Let's go look at the gardens in the back."

"Mom didn't kill herself," I said the moment the door closed and we were alone. "It was an accident. A cop who'd been there told me so." I kept remembering how I felt when Dad first told me she had possibly committed suicide, rehashing my anger to keep from crying.

He nodded his head but didn't say anything for several seconds. Then he backtracked and tried to cover for what he said.

"I didn't know if your mom tried to commit suicide or not, but it is true that she'd been depressed and was on medication...and that you wouldn't even give Abbie a chance."

I couldn't believe he had the nerve to even bring up Abbie in the same sentence as Mom. He stopped talking and looked down at the stains in the carpet.

"But I was right about Abbie," I said.

"I know," he whispered. "I was just so lonely."

"No. You're not going to use that as an excuse. Millions of people are lonely."

"I'm sorry," he said. It was the first time he'd said he was sorry about anything since Mom died. And because he hadn't said it until now; because he almost choked over each word as it came out, I believed he meant it.

"When your mom died, I wanted to go along with her, but I knew I needed to stick around for you and Joey." He was crying now. Big sloppy tears were rolling down his face and staining the front of his neatly pressed uniform shirt.

"I wanted to make Kathy sound worse than she was," he said between sobs. "I had to make myself believe it. It was the only way I could live without her."

After everything that had happened, all the crappy things he had done, I finally understood why. Most people made themselves believe that those in their lives who had passed on where more noble than they were. It eased the pain, softened difficult memories, and left behind a beautiful portrait. Mom wasn't perfect, but she'd been such an amazing person that he had to do the opposite to survive.

***

I turned fifteen on a Wednesday at the Hampton Hills Senior Living Community. Grandma threw me a party in the recreation room and invited a bunch of her old people friends. It was a surprise party with people peeking out from behind chairs and curtains.

"Happy Birthday!" Bill White shouted. There were at least a dozen old people there, patting me on the back and singing happy birthday in scratchy, off-key voices. Joey and I were the only ones in the room under sixty.

There were balloons, cake, and candy, so Joey thought the whole thing was great. Grandma hardly ever let him eat anything sweet, except for fruit and Jello. He was shoveling spoonfuls of ice cream and cake in his mouth like he hadn't eaten in a week.

"How old are you again?" Shirley Epperson asked as she leaned down and stroked my hair. Old people were always hugging and touching younger people. They must have thought our youth would rub off and give them a few extra years.

"Fifteen," I said. I wanted to say something ridiculous, like ten or twenty-three just to see if she would believe me.

"Fifteen," she said as if it were the most magical word in the English language. "I remember when I was fifteen."

I could hardly believe that, especially when I knew she couldn't even remember how to get back to her own duplex half the time.

After the party I thanked Grandma for everything she'd done. It wasn't exactly how I had envisioned celebrating my birthday, but at least I wasn't celebrating at tent city.

A few days after the party, Vivica and her sister came to see me. As strict as Grandma was about so many things, I was surprised that she let me leave with them. They were taking me to the Lock-n-Save Storage Center to pick up a few things Grandma had put away before the bank had foreclosed on our house.

After we'd been there a few minutes and had unlocked the storage unit I finally worked up enough nerve to ask Vivica about Misha.

"I was just wondering, have you seen or heard anything about Misha lately?" I opened the box with our laptop, checking to make sure nothing was broken.

"Luke Kessler had a party last weekend and Misha was there with a junior from Northwood Hills High School." She hesitated, and then said, "I think they're going out."

I shrugged. "It doesn't really surprise me," I said. "It's not like I expected Misha to wait around for me." I took a deep breath to push all the pain back down inside.

He was just one more thing I had lost during the last year. But if there was anything I'd learned in the last eleven months it was how to enjoy people, things, even life itself, without expecting anything to go on forever.

Standing in the open garage of the storage unit, fingering through the remnants of my life, I couldn't help but admire Vivica and her sister. They had done so much for me, yet it didn't seem like much of an effort for them. Picking me up from parties at midnight, taking me to retrieve treasured possessions; it was no more of a chore for them than running to the convenience store.

"What's this?" Vivica asked. She picked up one of the Hummel figurines.

"It's a little Dutch boy staring down at a tulip," I said as if it were obvious. I also assumed that the intricate beauty and worth of the item should be obvious as well. She wrinkled her nose then wrapped it back in the tissue paper and put it back in the box.

I'd been so worried about saving Mom's artifacts, all the stray pieces of a grand puzzle I'd put back together someday. But as time went on, I knew they'd never fit back together. Things changed; I'd changed, and what something was worth was almost always relative. I took the computer and some of Mom's handmade jewelry, things I could actually wear or use. Everything else, including the Hummels, I donated to charity.

Chapter Twenty-Three

In September, heat fell like burning coal into a city already scorched by drought and record-breaking temperatures. I started my sophomore year at Fairfield amid the constant rush of rickety old fans and the overbearing smell of too many hormonal bodies sweating together in overcrowded rooms.

Vivica and I actually had three classes together. We sat in the same row in Social Studies, were lab partners in Science, and even had a study hall together. Her older sister had moved out of the house and was living with her boyfriend, but her Dad had a new girlfriend who didn't mind driving Vivica and me around wherever we wanted to go.

"I think he might even marry this one," she whispered during study hall.

I figured she'd be more excited. She'd finally have some stability in her life, but she didn't seem very happy about it.

"I thought you liked her," I said. "Don't you want them to get married?"

She shrugged. "I like her. It's just that my dad has been single for so long now I think it would be weird if he actually got married again."

People were creatures of habit and didn't want to try something new, even if the potential was there for something better.

After study hall I went to lunch. Vivica and I weren't in the same lunch period so I usually sat with the band kids, which meant Misha sat at our table. I still liked him, and we talked every now and then, but I realized after he dumped me off that I wasn't ready for a boyfriend like Misha. He seemed so much older and experienced than most of the other high school kids, even the ones in my old homeroom who had bragged about doing all kinds of crazy things.

Misha was going out with a girl who had moved to Fort Wayne from Texas over the summer. She was beautiful, but barely spoke any English. I had a feeling Misha liked it that way.

I glanced over at the next table and saw Mary Frances. Her red curly hair was longer this year, hanging down over her eyes. But from where I was sitting, I could still see those pearly white teeth and that impish grin. Since Mary Frances and I didn't have any classes together I rarely talked to her anymore.

Overall, this year was starting out pretty good. I liked most of my classes and had made quite a few friends in the band. Thankfully, I hadn't made any new enemies this year. Even Dani wasn't around anymore. Supposedly, she beat up a clerk in a convenience store during the summer and had been sent to ACJC until the end of October. I didn't really care if she came back to Fairfield or not. I'd already settled my score with her last year. But her reputation as a merciless beast had grown even stronger in her absence. Sometimes I overheard the new kids talking about her in the restroom or during lunch with a sense of awe and reverence reserved for mythical figures.

I never did find out what happened to Tara. For all I knew she got a placement with a nice family living in a good school district. She was smart enough to go to college and actually end up making something of herself. On the other hand, I could see her running away, joining a gang and ending up in women's prison by eighteen. With Tara the possibilities were endless.

At the end of the day I made my way through tangles of kids to the front entrance where Dad was waiting for me.

"How was your day?" he said as I climbed into the car.

"Okay," I said.

"Do you have much homework?"

I shook my head. He turned the radio on after that. He was trying to get to know me again and be part of my life, but it didn't come easy.

A steady stream of kids were still pouring out of the building, weaving their way between the cars, and holding up traffic in the parking lot.

Dad had been out of rehab for a little over a month now. He'd been back at work for a few weeks and we were living in an apartment less than a mile from my school.

"Are you sure you still want to go?" he said.

I nodded without looking at him. As he pulled out of the parking lot I rolled down the window.

It was almost the one year anniversary of Mom's death and I'd asked him to take me to her grave. Dad was going to drop me off and then pick up Joey from school. That would give me about half an hour before they came back to get me.

He didn't say anything else about going to the cemetery the rest of the way there. He complained about the traffic and honked when some old guy cut him off.

As soon as he pulled into the entrance, I told him to stop. "I'll get out here," I said.

"Are you sure? I can drive back farther."

"It's a nice day. I want to walk."

He nodded. "I'll be back after I get Joey."

I waited until he drove out before I started walking. I didn't want to share even a small part of this experience with anyone. Lindenwood was an old Catholic cemetery full of large Oak and Elm trees. There were Maples that were already starting to turn color; fire red, bright yellow, and deep plum.

As I walked through the cemetery, I noticed several other people there. Some were laying wreaths and flowers on the graves while others were staring intently into the headstones.

An old lady was standing in front of a grave about twenty yards away from my mother's. She looked like she was at least eighty, maybe older, and she was crying hysterically, asking Charles why he had to leave her after sixty years. She'd lost someone at that age and was complaining? I knew enough now to realize that death was a kick in the face at any age, but still, I thought she had a lot of nerve yelling at him when what they had was probably the best anyone could hope for in this life.

When I finally got to the grave, I stared at the dusty gray headstone, still shiny and new compared to most of the others. I hadn't brought anything to leave there, only a part of myself. But that was all my mother would have wanted.

I knew I'd finally made it across my Red Sea. The waters were closing behind me, drowning all the obstacles and fears that had held me down for nearly a year. But it also meant I could never go back. I'd never be the person I was before.

I knew her early departure would affect me for the rest of my life. But in spite of everything that had happened, our lives were almost normal again. Since watching my dad turn into a drunk, losing our home, and knowing I'd almost faded away and then came back as someone I'd never known before, almost normal was the best I could hope for.

Made in the USA
Monee, IL
16 April 2022